METAGESTURES

Fig. 1. Hieronymus Bosch, *Ship of Fools* (1490–1500)

First published in 2019 by punctum books, Earth, Milky Way.
https://punctumbooks.com

ISBN-13: 978-1-950192-25-0 (print)
ISBN-13: 978-1-950192-26-7 (ePDF)

DOI: 10.21983/P3.0253.1.00

LCCN: 2019940254
Library of Congress Cataloging Data is available from the Library of Congress

Book Design: Vincent W.J. van Gerven Oei

HIC SVNT MONSTRA

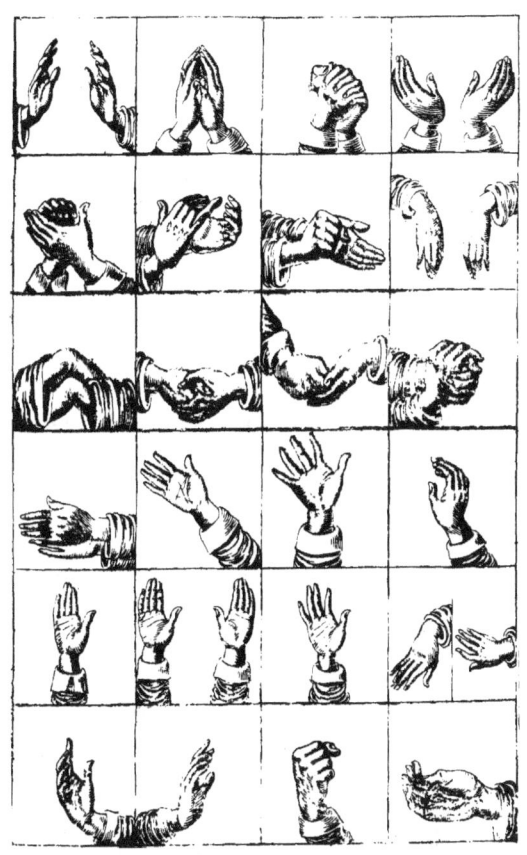

METAGESTURES

Carla Nappi & Dominic Pettman

CARLA NAPPI

Dominic Pettman

Introduction:
The Gesture of
Introducing

Writing

To do anything is to bring something about, to make possible a first meeting, if we let it be. All of Flusser's gestures — writing, speaking, making, destroying, painting, photographing, filming, turning a mask around, planting, shaving, listening to music, smoking a pipe, telephoning, video, searching, loving — are ultimately also gestures of introducing.

We had both independently been writing books inspired by the same strange small work of fiction, and there we were at Cabinet Magazine's Brooklyn headquarters for the second time (now as Dominic and Carla rather than Horse and Phoenix) and we had woven our two Calvino-inspired projects into a third monstrous beautiful thing and somehow people had come to hear us offer it to the room. There was something about the fact of sitting at a table in front of a group of people, and bodily bringing a thing made of language to them, and doing that together. Doing it together somehow brought something new to the pieces we were presenting and to the language itself. Writing had become a way of introducing ourselves to Calvino, and to each other, and now to the possibility of writing together.

Speaking

We have to do this again!, I said. What about Flusser's *Gestures*?, he said.

Making

One by one we began to read the chapters of Flusser's book. There were no rules, except for an agreed-upon-and-highly-fungible deadline for our responses to each gesture. We'll each take the same object as our anchor, and we'll each write our way into engaging with the parts of it that most inspire us as individuals, and we'll just make something, we decided, and by making and then sharing what we've made we'll introduce ourselves and each other to the project. We both began to make little fictions. (We hadn't explicitly decided to do that. It just happened that way.) And, gradually, tiny ephemeral worlds upon gestural worlds began to come into being.

And gradually our fictions began to inspire and inform each other.

Destroying

Sometimes I worry about the potential violence done to each gesture in the act of creating a fictional world with it. I sometimes strip Flusser's writing to its bones and remake another text with those bones. It's a way of getting inside a piece, destroying it in order to introduce myself to it, breaking it in order to make with it. (Mostly I don't worry about this.)

Painting

"The gesture of painting is a form of freedom," Flusser tells us. He urges us "to try to look at the world with fresh eyes, without the prejudicial spectacles of objectification and abstraction that come with our tradition. Then the world would 'appear' again, illuminated with the splendor of concrete phenomena" (70–71).

Fictioning, for us, gradually became a way of paying attention anew. It became a practice that helped us to see Flusser's theory with fresh eyes, and to find a way across the flesh of it by creating languaged-hands to feel its languaged-body.

Every gesture is a gesture of introducing.

Photographing

Every gesture is a gesture of introducing.

So Dominic and I began to remake Flusser's gestures, using them as a kind of material stuff to create with, reimagining our respective worlds and populating them with invented gestural beings. Sometimes Dominic and I make gods. Sometimes factory-workers, or birds, or angels, or people who can inhabit each other's bodily experiences. Sometimes earthworms made of fingers, or storytellers who live in parks and drink green tea. Sometimes we make vampires who feed on color. Sometimes the bodies of the people we make help re-introduce me to my own body. (The woman who emerged from my response to Flusser's "Photographing" introduced me to my fingertips anew. You'll see what I mean when you meet her. The Mr. in Dominic's response introduced me to my eyes anew. You'll see when you meet him.)

Always each of us has been experimenting with fiction as part of our practice of engaging theory, and of making lives with it, individually and together.

Filming

Flusser describes cinema as "the archetypal womb" (86). Filming is a kind of bringing-into-being, a way of creating the possibility of history. It's a gesture of imagining on a surface, which is ultimately what we're doing as well.

Fictioning with Flusser has been a way to read ourselves into the subterranean of each gesture. (Sometime we read together, in real time, sending each other wordphotos of the bones or fossils or gems we find in the course of our digging, and sharing them, and helping each other see what we otherwise might have lost in the soil.) We then each write our own way back out again, making new surfaces to project imagination onto.

Turning a Mask Around

It's a physical act, writing. Every time I open my file and think myself into a gesture and try to find a way to inhabit it, it becomes a way of re-introducing theory to its own latent nature as a raw material for storytelling, my own gestural body to a transcendent space of imagined sensoria, my worldmaking gesture to that of a beloved collaborator and his to mine. (Every gesture is a gesture of introducing.) It's always a coming-together, a way of being-there and being-with.

Planting

While each of the stories in this book was inspired directly by a close reading of the corresponding gesture in Flusser's book, the connections between the source material and the story growing from it are not always apparent. We thought long and carefully about how to approach this in the book. In making an offering of stories to you, our readers, should we be making explicit the connections between the stories and the bits of Flusser's text that inspired them? (Should we be showing you photos of the early budding stages of the flowers as they grew?) Should we be framing each story with a map showing you how to get (showing you how we got) from A to B?

In the end, we decided not to. True to the spirit of how we read Flusser, we are treating each of these stories as a kind of gestural act that creates its own space, its own world, and invites you to come dwell within it and see what comes. You might choose to read each collection of stories independently before moving on to the other, or you might flip the book over after each reading and experience the stories in pairs, as they were written. At the same time, there is yet another way of reading this book. You might find yourself a copy of Flusser's *Gestures* and slowly read each gesture before turning to the two stories in this book that were inspired by it. None of these ways of reading are right or wrong: in each case, something different will grow out of the experience.

Shaving

It is important that the stories — even as they live in different halves of the book — are in pairs. Each pair of stories — each set of gestures of shaving, or telephoning, or searching — was written in the same extended moment, springing from the same (sometimes quite brief, sometimes very extended) conversation. By binding them together in a single book, we honor the process and movements that made them. Each pair was born together, even as the stories often grew into quite different individuals.

Listening to Music

In the stories to come in this half of the book, you'll find common chords. Flesh will transform, bodies will come together and come apart. Much of what I drew from Flusser's work on gesture was, ultimately, about the way movement in space makes selves, and the perceptions thereof mark themselves on the meat of us, and spark metamorphoses, and turn the matter of us into the matter we perceive.

Smoking a Pipe

Fictioning with Flusser's work became a way to read Flusser. And so, writing became a way of learning how to read. It became a way of understanding that Flusser's reflections on the gesture of smoking a pipe were not necessarily about smoking, not were they necessarily about pipes. Instead, they could be about the importance of the act of recognition of the other, and of oneself in the other.

Every gesture is a gesture of introducing.

Telephoning

In fictioning with Flusser's work — and in fictioning together with Dominic — gesture, for me, became fundamentally about physicality. To gesture was to gesture with the aid of some sort of an apparatus. Sometimes, as in the gesture of telephoning, that apparatus became a "melancholy witness" to unfolding events. Sometimes we need to break off a piece from it and hold it to our ears to hear what it wants to tell us about what it has witnessed. Sometimes, when we listen, we hear our own voices. And sometimes we hear the voices of gods, be they gods already formed, or gods in the process of becoming. And thus, in fictioning with Flusser's work, physicality became inextricably linked with the relationship between self and gods. Do not be surprised, then, if you find gods of all sorts in the stories to come.

Video

The objects in the stories to come are troubled and troubling. They are often in the process of metamorphosis, of coming into and going out of focus, of forming and unforming. Voices, banjos, mouths and fingers, spiders and worms, statues, plants, rocks and beds and sheets of glass.

SEARCHING

To be an object, here, is to be sought. To be a subject is to search. To search is to suffer, and it is to beckon to the distance. It is to be passionate and to perceive. It is to realize that we are all gestures, projecting ourselves into the future as it projects itself upon us.

Fictioning with Dominic and with Flusser has been a way to realize that all reading is potentially an act of searching, and all searching is an act of fictioning.

LOVING

And so, we have made beings and fashioned worlds for them to inhabit. Sometimes the entities we make re-introduce us to ourselves, or to each other. (Every gesture is a gesture of introducing.)

You'll meet us, in a way, by meeting our gardeners and photographers and painters and lovers in these pages. (Maybe you'll meet yourselves there, also.) Gesture by gesture, we'll transform, and perhaps you will as well, and new introductions will have to be made. We will be planting, and shaving, and listening to music, and smoking a pipe, and telephoning, and videoing, and searching along with Flusser. We will be thinking gestures beyond Flusser, and inventing worlds with them, gestures made with ankles and elbows and eyebrows, beckonings and refusings and spinnings and offerings and brushings, or perhaps none of these at all. In the meantime, here is an ending. Here is a beginning. It's nice to meet you.

Introduction:
The Gesture of
Introducing

This introduction is a mediated gesture, *in medias res,* designed to help you, dear reader, become better acquainted with the writings that comprise this book; how they originated, and what they are attempting to achieve. I cannot see your facial expression while I am doing the introducing, so I do not have a sense of whether my gesture is capturing your attention. Perhaps it is boring you, or having some other effect that I did not even anticipate. (Perhaps you have already thrown the book out a window, starting a chain of events that will require further gestures from you in future, to avoid a law suit.) And because I cannot get a real-time "read" on the facility of my gesture, I have to put my faith in these ink-dried words to perform the magical alchemy described below. This gesture thus comes with a subtextual incantation: a spell encouraging a greater familiarity with the project, and thus — hopefully — a sympathetic orientation towards it.

All gestures hover somewhere between an action and an intention: not as fully realized or instrumental as the former, but nor as inchoate or tentative as the latter. Gestures are a kind of somatic language within which we inhabit. They thus create an impersonal syntax, even as these are performed with our singularized, idiomatic bodies. This is the paradox: gestures are "public domain," as it were, and part of our cultural inheritance; and yet they can also be highly individual or idiosyncratic. They can be required (the soldier's salute) or unexpected (the lover's seduction). As such, gestures inhabit the zone between agency and instinct, expression and reflex, freedom and automaticity.

The gesture of introducing—like most of the gestures described by Vilém Flusser in the book that inspired this project—is ubiquitous and, because of this, almost subliminal. We introduce things every day, or are introduced to them. And yet we are so focused on the subject or object being introduced that we miss the gesture that allowed it to happen. (Or, at most, we register it on an unconscious level.) The only time a quotidian gesture becomes conspicuous is when it is performed badly, or draws attention to itself for some theatrical or ironic reason. A good gesture, in the modern era, is one which happens so organically that it is barely noticed by those within its subtle, yet decisive, orbit. (Flusser describes it as "covered up by habit"; a case of "hyperfamiliarity.") Such a gesture allows an action to occur, but the action itself comprises the prime interest.

Many have railed against the standardization of our gestures in modern times, and the subsequent alienation this is said to provoke. (Our smartphones, for instance, are teaching us to make specific and unprecedented gestures in order to communicate with them.) Flusser noted that there is no such thing as a free gesture, in our contemporary world. However, there *is* something like freedom expressed within it. It seems that gestures — like information — want to be free. Indeed, this subliminal aspect of gestural life may be one of the ways we measure the distance, and difference, between the modern age and that which came before. Modernity demands elliptical, automatic, and standardized gestures. We may even call them algorithmic, considering how pre-programmed they have become, following cultural scripts in a way designed to minimize acknowledgement of their rather arbitrary forms, ideological interests, and performative roots. Before the modern age (so the story goes, at least), gestures existed more for their own sake. There was an elaborate dramaturgy (and comedy) of expressive manners and movements. The body was freer — at least in comparison to today — to make gestures untethered to limiting factors such as age, gender, class, or profit margin. (Though a medieval serf, obliged to toil in the fields all day may take umbrage at such a narrative.) Gestures were not an index of one's calcified identity, but rather identity was presumed to emerge rather loosely from one gesture to the next. If these gestures contradicted themselves, they created less social dissonance, since personal coherence was not the foundation for public interactions. Rather one adopted different roles for each context, one threaded together with the other by the explicit self-referencing work of the gestures themselves. (Once again, a rather Romantic historical distinction, but one with at least a grain of truth to it.)

In any case, in premodern times, gestures were more easily recognized as such, and performed with more autopoetic aplomb. Think of the gestures of courtly love — the elaborate bows and curtsies, as well as all the motions and emotions involved in delivering secret amorous messages. The medium here, long before McLuhan, was the message. It meant less what the poem conveyed, than the heart-sick knight convey the poem with suitably legible and emphatic gestures. Today, in contrast, the less detectable the romantic gesture, accomplished via an expressionless mouse-click or text message, the more likely it is to succeed. In short, the gesture — itself presumed to be one of the ways in which the human departs from the animal — became less and less a sign pointing to itself (as if to say: "Attention. Humanity at work!"), and more and more an ambient cue or direction, withdrawn into the wider environment, allowing the work of the human to proceed without reflection or objection. (According to this logic, Italians are yet to fully enter the modern era.)

Let us return, then, to the gesture of introducing. In keeping with the modern/premodern conceit; in days of yore, the introduction of one person to another (or one person to a group), involved a rather complex understanding, orchestral command, of elements including the birth, station, social trajectory, ambition, and potential valences of the people being introduced. If the gesture were not suitably baroque and garrulous, then the new acquaintance would risk cracking, like a glass-blown vase, taken too soon out of the furnace. Today's newly forged relationships are no less burdened by the elements listed above, but these must under no circumstances be explicitly acknowledged. The person charged with the gesture of introducing is no longer a master of ceremonies, but rather an usher of supreme discretion, or an agent charged with making a swift and quiet connection between assassins in a public place. Identities must be affirmed, of course. But the new relationship must not be considered of a different kind, cloth, or quality to any other. In the modern age, all relationships are equally important (and thus equally trivial), at least in theory. (Being introduced to a celebrity or VIP thus retains powerful pre-modern resonances.) The gesture of introducing officiates over a formal ceremony of transformation — turning strangers into acquaintances. However, as we've already noted, the gesture cannot be too formal. It cannot draw attention to itself, lest it risk the ease of this transformation. The gesture of introduction should thus be an embodiment of ease; a kind of subtle social alchemy.

But we do more than just introduce people to other people. We also introduce people to notions, possibilities, concepts, and ideas. When introducing such nebulous things to others, the gesture becomes more performative again, retaining those pre-modern traces of volubility. Think of the professor at the lectern, or pacing the stage, deploying an entire repertoire of gestures, borrowed from the public bank of intellectualized hand motions, to trace the contours of mental activity and exploration. We also introduce others to objects and things. Once again, this gesture is also more atavistic than when introducing our fellow men and women to each other, probably because it is beholden to the fetishistic power of the commodity. Things, perhaps ironically, retain a residue of enchantment, before the world was sandblasted by secularistic materialism. Even objects as common and banal as those found in Walmart or Ikea lay claim to some kind of agency or aura, thanks to the transitive powers of advertising. And thus, the gesture of introducing an object ("Behold, the new iPhone") is supremely self-conscious; the grimace of the model on *The Price Is Right*, introducing an expensive barbecue set, or the smug pucker of the tech-entrepreneur, strutting around on a stage like some kind of turtle-necked courtier, in charge of acquisitions. (And it will truly be a sign of our ultimate assimilation of technology when we introduce new platforms and gadgets with the "cool" insouciance adopted when introducing humans to other humans.)

Indeed, we introduce people to many other things besides. Places. Spaces. Art works. Lifestyles. Secrets. The list goes on. One of the most cherished gestures amongst literary types like myself, is introducing someone to a beloved author. I was first introduced to Vilém Flusser's work by another book I was reading, and I am eternally grateful to the author of this book for making our acquaintance, for Flusser's words have changed the way I see the world (including the way I see words themselves). Sometimes delayed gestures, performed across both time and space, are the most consequential.

Moreover, one of the other most cherished gestures — once again, amongst literary types — is being introduced to a beloved co-author. I was first introduced to my collaborator, Carla Nappi, by the editor of a cultural magazine in New York City. This editor had organized an event at a major art museum, in which 26 people gave a mini-lecture about 26 different animals, arranged in order from smallest to largest. I re-introduced the horse to this audience, and Carla reintroduced the phoenix. Upon this first meeting, we discovered we were both in the midst of manuscripts inspired by Italo Calvino. And a few months later, we even presented our works to the world, now entangled through some hasty yet ingenious stitching operations. We then turned to Flusser as our muse, as he challenged us to really *observe* and *consider* the gestures that we so often take for granted, or with a pinch of salt. (We so often, for instance, talk of the photographer or the photograph, forgetting completely to take account of the *gesture of photographing* which connects these two icons of the art world.)

Which is to say that perhaps the most consummate and exquisite gestures are the ones performed by the cosmos itself, rather than by the people who presume they are the sole authors or executors of these events. For when the universe introduces something into the flow of life, or the fabric of the situation, it does so without fanfare or warning. And then withdraws silently to watch what unfolds.

THE GESTURE OF
WRITING

After getting barely any sleep Vilém sprung awake, flew out the door, thought better of it, doubled back, tidied up his nest, fluffed the pillows, brushed away stray bits of twig and tinsel, speed-walked back to the door, locked it behind him, and began his day.

This was a day unlike others. He breezed by friends and neighbors — greeting them, perhaps, with a high-pitched whinny or a buzzy bobolinky whistling or a *cha-cha-lac* — as he rushed to the telegraph station.

When he arrived he threw open the door and called out to the tuxedoed station manager with his most urgent trilling song. Understanding immediately, and half in shock at the news, the manager quickly pushed a sheet of staff paper and a pen at the other man, stood up, brushed off coat and tails, and proceeded to the piano. When Vilém had finished with his message, he put down the pen and brought the note-spattered sheet to the manager in his new position on the piano bench. That man quickly scanned the half and quarter and eighth notes scrawled on the page, *fe-bree*'d out a brief question, listened for Vilém's quacking reply, flexed his fingers, and began to play.

First, the station manager pounded out the code for the appropriate receiving station. As he continued to play, with each note or chord struck on the piano the corresponding keys tapped a series of wires translating it to the other station. There, a player piano sitting on standby *plink*ed and *plonk*ed to life as its keys began mimicking the notes of the manager. Its sharps and flats and naturals connected to a system of levers and inks and gears and by the conclusion of the message a thin sheet of staff paper nearly identical to that which Vilém had handed over was extruded from its side.

Once it was done, Vilém honked a thank-you and retreated to a corner of the station to pace and flutter as the manager sped back to his desk in a rush of black and white and awaited a reply. Minutes later, an open-backed banjo mounted under the desk began to pluck out a series of notes in a clawhammer style. As the strings self-strummed, they grooved the paper mounted on the fretboard beneath them, and while the tuxedoed manager quickly read the fretmarks he furiously inked clefs and notes and beams and rests while Vilém looked on and *twee-twee*d in panic and the banjo *twang*ed and the manager scribbled and listened and so did Vilém as he shuffled to the desk and it was *twang*-groove-*twee*-scribble-shuffle *twang*-groove-*twee*-scribble-shuffle until, with a phantom drop-thumb, the banjo ceased its message and so did the fretboard and so did the manager and he stared at the paper and then looked up at Vilém and handed him the translation and exhaled and collapsed into a chair.

Vilém read, and his emotions were written on his face by the twisting of ropy eyebrows and the pull of flesh and hair around his nose and chin. Eyes and skin and nostrils gathered into a text on which the station manager read despair. Seeing this, the manager pulled his fear into himself and unfolded his body and dusted off his jacket and went once again to sit at his piano. Without a script to render and not quite knowing what to say, he tuned the instrument to broadcast to all stations, he placed his fingers, and he began to strike the keys. Knowing what was coming — and coming soon — the manager wrote for his life. He played from the beginning — from his first memories in his parents' nest — and as he played he came to understand, and even as his knuckles cramped and his fingertips bloodied the station manager began to smile, and the warbling behind him faded to an echo, and he knew that it was not going to be alright, but that was alright, and he closed his eyes and kept playing.

THE GESTURE OF
WRITING

How long must a trace remain before it can count as an inscription? And what kinds of inscription count as writing? (Can one even "count" writing? Or is that to confuse the alphabetical with the mathematical?) When the fox leaves prints in the snow, might this be an unplanned narrative, its pace and meaning depending on the reader (a fellow mammal, most likely)? Can a dog sniff a good story — full of nuanced gossip — in the urine of an absent canine author — one who specializes in slim volumes of liquid free-verse on fire-hydrants? Alternatively, the lazy, rippling wake of a sampan in the Perfume river — might this be a fleeting story of something? A prosaic record of passage on the glittering surface of water? Photography claims to write in light, just as phonography tells tales in sound. These are modes of capture. And exposure.

Many claim that writing is an exclusively human gesture, achieved through machinic means, and with inhuman materials. Others, however, insist that the inky traces we leave in books, on walls, and scraps of paper are essentially no different from the slime which a snail leaves in sticky memory of its sluggish trail.

***

The old writer yawned, as his red-rimmed eyes tried to adjust to the bright early afternoon light. He sipped on a misshapen ceramic cup, filled with Japanese green tea, so strong that it tasted like tobacco mixed with algae, mashed and diluted into a thin paste. (A habit he acquired during a working visit in the East, many years ago.) Lately the old writer had been composing long poems about nature. And he had come to believe that the words on the page were at least partly excretions of the organic materials he absorbed in order to function in the first place. Writing came as natural to him as breathing; perhaps even more so. (Many times, he had been accused by friends or former lovers as being little more than a "word processor": a man-machine who would rather hammer out some detailed account of an imagined experience than enjoy or suffer a real one.) But in each subsequent sip of his bitter tea, the old writer could also taste the chemicals which leeched into the soil, and thus — eventually — into the soul. Nature was receding from him. And his prose felt less and less effective at trapping and tagging it.

The old writer peeked his rather hairy head out of the little wooden hut the authorities had provided, loosely modeled on Thoreau's modest dwelling near Walden pond. There was no body of water nearby, however. Just a 30-foot perimeter, enclosing rather featureless shrubs and anonymous landscaping. A young Russian couple were standing on the other side of the railing, facing the other way, so did not see him. They were taking a photograph of themselves with a camera, perched on the end of a long silver-stick, designed for that purpose. Sticks, the old writer reflected, were a technology that would always find a purpose. Sticks for scratching. Sticks for stabbing. Sticks for hitting. Sticks for walking. Sticks for writing.... Sticks of incense, for worship. Sticks of dynamite, for warships. *Sticks and stones may break the bones, but words can never hurt us*. Only children could say such a thing; disproving their own point by repeating the mantra to waxy, offended ears. *The pen is mightier than the sword*. Equally untrue, when it comes down to it.

After eating some grains and fruit, and suffering the abrasive evacuations that followed, he put on his wide-brimmed hat and ventured out into the sun. More tourists were now gathered against the railing, several feet above him, and made clicking noises with their mouths and cameras at his appearance. The old writer had long ago given up the habit of acknowledging the clients of the park, who came to see those last remaining people who work outside the Apparatus — those like himself, who (for instance) write as a mode of expression, rather than as a function. The old writer was, in fact, one of twelve different writers in the Park, and the father of two of them. The authorities had, once upon a time, used him, and his once-potent plume, in the hope of continuing the line of this endangered species. But those days were now long gone, as this honor went to younger, more virile wordsmiths. (Itself an interesting concept: a "wordsmith" — like a blacksmith, perhaps? — who forges elaborate communicational shapes on a sparking mental anvil, out of the malleable materials of molten language.... *To forge*: meaning both to create and to fake.)

The old writer shuffled down the short and narrow stone path to the gazebo, where his trusty typewriter rested (and rusted) on a bamboo table, upon which fresh paper was always waiting for him, compliments of the Park. He liked to refer to this beloved object as "the machine in the garden." (Just as the old writer was well aware that he himself was an inhabitant of one of the few remaining gardens in the wider world machine.) Now that the authorities had passed on their budget cuts, in the form of tomato juice spiked with apple vinegar, rather than the half-decent red wine he used to enjoy, his work was, admittedly, more focused. The first few months, after this unwelcome change, were ugly. He refused to write, until an unblinking woman of indeterminate age and accent convinced him — by way of elaborate cajolings and expertly veiled threats — to start tapping away once more. The following weeks saw an angry torrent of words spew out of the typewriter, filled with violence and impotent rage. But no matter. No-one ever read what he wrote. And even if they did, these new people would have no idea what to make of such words, unfit for the so-called "living" documents of the new age.

(Documents only living in the same sense as the undead, according to the old writer.)

After a while, the tomato juice cocktail had its cleansing
effect on his internal organs, which themselves re-organized
themselves into an arrangement that no longer required self-
tranquilization to create. He felt more exposed to the invisible
elements of existence, and thus his writing became keener. Did
it bother him that he had no readers, only spectators or witnesses? If so, it did not show in his creative process. Nor in his mood,
which was mostly sanguine. Or at least, resigned. He was glad
they let him write. After all, what else could, or would, he do?

And so he sat in front of the typewriter, which — though
rusty — still clunked away faithfully, when pressed, like a beloved steam-train of childhood, that never left the station. He did
not write immediately, however. First he settled into his wicker
chair, with the old velvet cushion that had graciously adapted
to his rather moist and bony buttocks. (The days were usually
hot in the park, and even more so in the concrete bowls of the
exhibits.) Indeed, he would sit for hours and hours, without hitting a single key. This was his process. He would clear his mind
for an hour or so, while methodically and unthinkingly cracking
each of his knuckles. He would then pick up a piece of paper,
with a vain flourish, and wind it into the mechanism. (A gesture
which would often yield a smattering of applause from the onlookers.) These same onlookers would then become impatient,
as he would continue to stare and ponder — his fingers resting on the keys, like a concert pianist — without applying any
pressure. On occasion, some rude and impatient guests would
even throw things at him — pens, a lot of the time. Or peanuts.
Thankfully this type of action would usually get a swift reaction
from the guards, even if they often missed the teenagers spitting
gum in his thinning hair.

Were the visitors more literate, they would possibly pay more
attention to the signs informing them that the old writer was
virtually nocturnal; not actually creating words until the dusk.
For words tend to resist being written. They are themselves shy,
and would prefer to float on the tip of tongues than arrested on

the page. They shun the light, and gain confidence in the dark. So the old writer must coax them forth. In that sense, writing is something akin to a religious ritual, in which the spirits must be encouraged to show themselves, and linger. Then again, if asked, the old writer would no doubt consider such an analogy to be a touch too grandiose. The process may indeed include some of the intermediary gifts (or tricks) of the "medium," but also the simple focus of the child, determined to catch fireflies in a jar.

Which is why nights were best for writing, even as it annoyed the owners of the Park, since the visitors would never see the old writer actually involved in his vocation. And what's more, his tapping would keep the other exhibits awake — the artists, the lovers, the buskers, the waiters, the philosophers, the anarchists, the priests, the astrologers, the illusionists, the burlesque dancers, the professors, the match-makers, the raconteurs. *Tap-tap-tap. Ding. Swoosh.* The machine in the garden would clickety-clack its own language beyond the sputtering candle's reach, and into the darkness, like some kind of skeletal Victorian robot, seeking the last of its own species to court. After a while, the authorities trained a strong spotlight on the old writer's desk, which encouraged an army of moths to swirl around him. For weeks, the stories would stutter themselves into being, accompanied by the flutter of wings in his hair, ears, and eye-lids, and sometimes the crunchy dust of vibrating bodies in his mouth. (Those nights he sometimes dreamed sweet dreams of exotic women, tempting him to nibble on surprisingly bitter halva.) But one night the bulb of the spotlight died, and no-one remembered to replace it. And the old writer was typing by candle-light once more.

Writing and typing. Typing and writing. Until the sky began to brighten again. And the stars would wink away, one-by-one, taking the words of the night with them. Until there were no more willing to appear. Just a string of translucent letters in the air, curling and dissipating like smoke; fluttering elsewhere. Like moths.

At which time, the old writer would finally let the machine cease its rickety racket. And cover it, as if for sleep. Then shuffle back to his hut, just as the keepers of the Park were hosing down the pavements, in preparation for the next round of visitors.

THE GESTURE OF
SPEAKING

In the beginning was Ooooooooooooh.

And then came Uuhhhhhhmmmmmmmmm. And so there were Ooooooooooooh and Uuhhhhhhmmmmmmmmm.

And after some time, Ooooooooooooh and Uuhhhhhhhmmmmmmmmm made Ohhhmmmmmmmmm.

And they came together and throats and lips formed around them. And so there were Ooooooooooooh and Uuhhhhhhmmmmmmmmm and Ohhhmmmmmmmmm and throats and lips and then the lips made Ewwwwwwwwww and the throats made Aaaaaaaaahhhhhhh and then tongues formed around the Aaaaaaaaahhhhhhh and soon palates grew above them and so there were Ooooooooooooh and Uuhhhhhhmmmmmmmmm and Ohhhmmmmmmmmm and Ewwwwwwwwww and Aaaaaaaaahhhhhhh and throats and lips and tongues and palates and then came Lllllllaaaaaaaaaa and Mooooooo.

And they made more sounds, and gradually other parts formed around those, too, and this is how the world was made.

And after a while the parts came together—they were held together by the Ooooooooooooh and Uuhhhhhhmmmmmmmmm and Ohhhmmmmmmmmm and Ewwwwwwwwww and Aaaaaaaaahhhhhhh and Lllllllaaaaaaaaaa and Mooooooooo and the others — and as they moved together they began to make more sounds. And these huddles of parts and sounds learned that if they were to keep moving, they needed to make a common space to move in. And to do that they began to send sounds towards each other. And they found that if they did that, then those sounds made more sounds, and then they began to grow new parts around those new sounds.

And after a time, there were thumbs and lungs and knees and eyebrows.

(Some were born without thumbs, and these were the silent ones who sang no language and made no music, and in the same moment that they came into being, they hushed back into nothingness again.)

They lived together in a space made by the sounds, and that space flowed into them and they breathed it back out again and it was that way for a while. But one day, one of them reached out his arm and down through the bones and the sinews to the tips of his fingers he sent one of the sounds. Meeeeeeeeeeeeee, he shot through his veins and out his fingernails and into the space before him, and in doing so he changed that space. Once he realized what he had done, he did it again, and again, as sounds flowed from his toes and out his nostrils and through his throat, his lips, his mouth. (When he sent them out from his mouth he could stop them and chew them and tongue them and he liked that, so he kept doing that over and over.) Others saw him, and heard him, and gradually tried to do it themselves. And they learned how the different sounds tasted, and they stirred the sounds together in their mouths — a kind of soundcooking — to make new tastes and they blew them at one another and tasted each other's sounds and they were nourished. And they came to believe that they had harnessed the sounds, and taken control of the spaces, and they cooked words together or ate them raw and they built structures out of their sounds and moved through them and continued to trust in their power as chefs and as architects and they forgot where their flesh came from, forgot that the sounds had made their lips, that their throats and bellies had formed around the sounds, and they forgot themselves. And so they didn't understand when the Lllllllaaaaaaaaaaa left, and the Ohhhmmmmmmmmmm stopped coming, and the Ewwwww- wwwww and the Aaaaaaaaaahhhhhhhh grew tasteless, and then there was no more to chew, and the structures dissolved, and as the sounds went silent, one by one the parts that they sustained began to disappear — the knees, and the nostrils, and the eye- lids, and the lips, and the tongues, and the rest. As the last one reached his arm out again for the last time, he tried to scratch a Meeeeeeeeeeeeee into the dust as his fingernails crumbled and his skin dried and powdered away and all he was were eyes and bones until those crumbled, too. And it made no sound, and the rest was silence.

THE GESTURE OF
SPEAKING

Nell abhorred the gesture of speaking. As a result, she spoke as little as the world would allow her to. As a little girl, her teachers thought her dim, and possibly even mute; though she was neither. Perhaps unexpectedly, she was popular with the other girls, by virtue of her aversion to self-expression. Thus she found herself — much against her will or wishes — befriended by strident, skirted creatures who could not shut up for even a moment. It was all Nell could do to resist covering her ears in silent complaint.

Nell's parents despaired of their daughter's quiet introversion, never knowing what she really felt about anything. She never voiced a preference for toast or cereal, horses or bassoons, adventurers or poets. On one occasion, these concerned and good-natured souls sent Nell to a psychiatrist. The talking cure, however, was not the right route for a girl who seemingly gave her tongue to a cat, for the price of a pair of rather feline eyes. And so, after the poor professional had run out of his bag of solicitous tricks, his patient fell asleep on the couch. An expensive nap, to be sure.

At night, as the barn owl hooted in a tree outside her bedroom window, Nell would smile to herself, tingling with the pleasant sensation of all those pre-articulations swimming around in her bloodstream. Indeed, these unuttered things would give her the energy to hop, skip, and jump through the following day. (For it is a little known fact that unspoken words are rich in iron and potassium.)

As already mentioned, however, Nell was not technically mute. She would thus sometimes startle and alarm her family, friends, or teachers by allowing a word or two to escape from somewhere deep within the shrouded belfry of her silence. But these disappeared again so quickly that those within hearing range were inclined to suspect — once the fugitive syllables dropped back below the surface of her body, like so many heavy carp, plopping down deep once more into a lake — that they were suffering aural hallucinations. What's more, there seemed to be no special pattern to those rare moments when she let her vocal cords strum themselves into a linguistic vibration. They had no special significance or import. Perhaps, on such occasions the words themselves were curious to see what the world was like, outside the tranquil chamber of her rather aesthetic silences. Perhaps a batch of phonemes banded together in order to feel themselves glow, on the other side of the velvet curtain of her throat; tip-toing sometimes shyly, other times boldly, off the scarlet carpet of her tongue. The paparazzi of her social circle could never catch the gesture of Nell's speech in the act, given its invisibility.

Sometimes Nell would hum along with the popular songs on the radio, but never sing the lyrics. When particularly tired or stressed from too much homework, she responded to the chatter that her mother listened to on the publicly funded talk shows by covering her ears, as if the sound coming from the speakers were not reasoned discussion, but the inhuman hiss of static snakes, coiling on to the kitchen countertops. Nell dreamed of growing up to be a librarian, in the world's most strict library, and looked forward to *shooshing* patrons of all ages, races, shapes, and sizes. (For *shooshing* was certainly not a figure of speech, since it did not originate in the breast or the larynx, but thrust itself forward from in front of the voice box, like the quick and shallow pneumatic rush from domestic bellows.)

Even when no longer a child, Nell suspected that the animals were just like her: perfectly capable of speech, but almost never deigning to resort to such a vulgar mode of interaction. (Those people who, throughout Occidental history, overheard the cautious animals in hushed conversation were uniformly dismissed or committed, as drunks, liars, witches, or madmen.) As a young woman Nell started studying at university. She soon opted to do this via correspondence course, since during the few lectures she endured, she could not concentrate. Indeed, she blushed in sympathetic humiliation, listening to professors being obliged to resort to their mouths to transmit the great ideas of our kind. During this time Nell learned of a philosopher who famously insisted that if a lion could speak, we should not understand what the creature said. She secretly suspected that we *would* in fact understand such a prolix beast only too well, which is why the great cats so wisely employed their heavy tongues to lick the antelope blood off their paws. (Though at night, on the savannah, when the moon is full, and the hunt successful, one might possibly hear the great lioness tell the tale of her most recent kill as a grisly lullaby for the three curious cubs at her feet.)

To break up the monotony of her studies, Nell would go to an old flea-bitten cinema near the abandoned synagogue in the outskirts of her town. She chose this rather mournful and forsaken venue because it specialized in silent movies; the only sound being the toothless growl of an old organ on Friday nights, or the hacking cough of an old spectator. Here, she met a melancholic, and rather ageless, usher who appealed to her in his refusal to speak to customers, many of whom never failed to ask inane questions. (*All* questions, of course, appearing to Nell as inane.) Through body language alone, and the coy tactical syntax of hem, hair comb, necklace and neckline, she eventually seduced him near the coat check, while the attendant was smoking a cigarette in the alley. Nell was quickly appalled, however, to find that in the full throes of lust, the previously enigmatic usher tried to whisper specific, sordid words into her ears. (The same ears she soaped with vigor for the next seven days straight, in her evening bath.) The argument they shared, after emerging from the impromptu mattress assembled with the inexpensive coats of strangers, could have well used emphatic intertitles, as they gesticulated wildly, in the same style as the old movie, currently flickering on the screen to a room of scattered, watery, cataract-compromised eyes.

Indeed, to see Nell's anger and disappointment at this moment — to see her being so silently verbose — was to see the true secret of speech. To wit, this gesture has precious little to do with the larynx in fact. Nor the tongue or the teeth. For the cavern of the mouth — and the fleshy voice box, in which words are held captive (all the better to send into the world, needy and grasping) — are not the true organs of speech.

As the animals know, this true organ is the eyes.

A truth that Nell would spend many lonely years understanding in solitude. That is before finding another (yes — this tale has a happy ending), who similarly understood that the lips, the tongue, and the teeth, should be reserved for eating or loving. Two ways, to be sure, of naming the same gesture.

THE GESTURE OF MAKING

On particularly loud, wet nights they would each retreat from their respective roomsful of boom-musicking and loud-talking and appliance-noising wherever they were and gather in a quiet office building on the edge of town in the silence of a nothing-special seminar room with a large oval table. As they sat they flexed their hands and placed them on the table, and when each had done that, one snapped her fingers. Thus they became the mothers of monsters, absenting the remainders of themselves to transform into a society of hands. Thus the carnival was called to disorder. Step right up!

Here are the five-legged spiders. They burst forth one day from a pair of very fine flowered silk scarves wrapped around the stumps of two arms someone had planted in the ground in a garden bursting with basil plants. They think by weaving. Watch them work long threads of celery string and shaved carrots and parsley stems between themselves as they plot their escape back into the soil!

Here are the five-tentacled octopuses. They were born from an arm reef that grew in warm waters and if you look closely you can see them pulse and stretch alongside each other as they search for prey to hold and press and suck and know.

Here are the five-headed earthworms. They were found in a dumpster full of extra wrists and elbows, crawling up out of the rotten remains of a large heavy book. Look at them study a can of coffee, prodding and provoking as they worm through the grinds and spread them out in fractal patterns that spell the names of gods.

Here is the angel with five-feathered wings.

Here are the tree-women crowned with five branches.

Here is the mothman who grew from a candle made from arms that were coated in wax and lit and left. Watch as he sculpts a lover from a pile of ashes. Watch as she struggles away from his making.

Here are the egrets with thumbbeaks and knuckleeyes. Look as they poke at a pile of eggshells to shape them into their favorite faces.

Here are the dragons with long spiky backs, born on a rainy day as arms reached up to squeeze the clouds. See them swimming in a bowl of thumbtacks, bloodily shaping them into nest.

After some time, one by one the creatures turned to one another and offered a gift. A parsley scarf. The foot of a charcoal girl. A hard white smile. A little sharp slick red pillow. Each quietly accepted what was offered. And once that was done, monsters unmade and hands unfolded and palms opened out to the air, one snapped her fingers and each of the people got up and put on their coats and went back out into the rain.

THE GESTURE OF MAKING

Serge removed the old oven gloves that he stashed inside the electric meter box above the bicycle racks, put them over his stubby hands, and then yanked down on the sturdy chain which opened the rusty factory shutters. His heart was even heavier than the mechanism he was engaged with, as he knew this was the last time he would perform such an action. The factory had been ordered closed for several months, as the owners brought in yet more machines; only this time, to replace almost all of the workers. (The bosses had offered Serge an ongoing supervisor position, for his loyalty to the company. He had since decided, however, to take the early pension, rather than see his friends in the bar after work, already drunk at 5pm, and him with factory shavings still on his clothes.) Serge was always the first to arrive at work, soon after dawn in summer, or hours before the sun peeped over the horizon, in winter. Today was the last day of August, so he did not have to light the gas lanterns. Sunlight streamed through the windows and skylights in dusty shafts, illuminating the way to Serge's modest office, in which he supervised all the various units of the factory. This building spread itself all along the southbank of the city's north canal; divided by departments, and linked by rickety footbridges, and plumbing lines. The whole place creaked to itself. This was Serge's favorite part of the day; before the others arrived, with their chatter and clatter and cigarette smoke. Before the morning whistle, the factory felt like a giant ship, happily lost at sea, with no human cargo but the foreman himself, with his thick moustache, and large, cow-like eyes.

Serge made himself some strong coffee inside a little pot on his desk, Turkish style, and then began the task he had been dreading all night. Indeed, he had been dreading it for months, as he could see it looming. This task was to make the final accounting of the various departments, so that the bosses could match the correct machines with the correct products. For this factory — like all such places — made things. It made a lot of different things: all of them rather hard to define or display. This factory specialized in all those items which were not tangible; and thus could not be sold in stores. Nevertheless, this conglomeration of workshops forged a decent living for all those who toiled therein, as Serge lived during those times when people happily, and unthinkingly, made things other than commodities; other than objects. Indeed these things were other than actual *things*. Before the recent Great Shift in manufacturing — precisely in this materialistic direction — most of the world's products were not the kind that could be photographed, or carried upstairs, or thrown into the river. Rather they helped society move forward. They enabled the lubrication of human joints, minds, hearts, and spirits.

Serge spent longer than he usually did, whittling a pencil to a sharp point. So sharp, in fact, that the pencil could feasibly be used as a weapon. Perhaps it could be used to liberate the bad blood from the artery in the factory owner's neck. But Serge was too old to entertain such vengeful scenarios for long. And so he wearily turned to the planning book, filled with technical diagrams, data logs, employee records, and other company miscellany. He then sipped his coffee, and began to review the different departments.

First was the unit responsible for *making do*. They were an especially enterprising group of young men and women, who were the last to get the chop from the bosses, because they were so skilled at simply "getting by," with whatever resources were available to them. For nearly a century now, this highly disciplined group had been making do; helping their fellow citizens brave storms, soldier on, and endure whatever conditions they found themselves in. Serge had always considered this department to be especially inspiring; and after attending their department meetings (as he attended all such official gatherings, around the factory), he always felt he could subsequently *get by* — with whatever came to hand. What was even more impressive, was the fact that this unit had been making do by hand, up until the past year, when they were obliged to start sharing their work space with a clattering rack of Do-Makers, imported from Brazil. Why the bosses were satisfied with the *do* made by these contraptions was beyond Serge, since the quality could not hold a candle to the original hand-made making do.

Next was the unit for *making light.* These meetings were Serge's favorite, since they were full of levity, which helped balance his soul, prone as it was to melancholy. And no matter how gloomy the reports delivered to them from on high, this group had a wisecrack or a euphemism to make everyone laugh. What's more, for a group of high-spirited lads and lasses, they were surprisingly efficient. No matter how many heavy situations were fed to them via the factory assembly line — two tons, four tons…sometimes even eight tons — they would manage to make light of it.

By instinct Serge moved his finger to flip to the next division, the group responsible for making fun; but then he remembered they had already been merged with the making light workers — and not without casualties. No matter how many times he had tried to explain the difference to the powers that be — that *making light* is a response to a difficult situation, whereas *making fun* is a more active type of action, effectively creating something from nothing — the bosses insisted that these two units were redundant. And so, henceforth, after the merger, the work of both teams were hampered by what the psychologists call "the narcissism of minor differences." Productivity went down.

Far less fun was made (down even to war-time levels on some weeks). Predictably, however, those employees who were originally light-makers had an easier time of it. After all, they were used to taking the density out of things. In any case, both these subpopulations of the plant were in the habit of working with their hands. And they found a certain solidarity in teasing the witless new Make-Light machines, with their obnoxious fanning devices and slinking springs.

Next to be reviewed was the unit responsible for *making time.* They were masters of their craft; only six men and women in all, given how detailed and painstaking the work was, and how few people possessed the skills and training to engineer temporality properly. They could be spotted in the canteen by the special equipment that dangled by their necks from a thin gold chain: special optical instruments, designed to see the passing seconds more clearly; and special manipulative ones, to delicately force the flow of time into different directions; to create bubbles within its inevitable gushing, filled with a different kind of continuousness. Serge had a soft spot for Eva, the most experienced of the workers in this unit, whose nimble hands were so deft at creating spare moments for others, but seemingly incapable of making any for herself (at least when Serge asked if she had any, so that he could take her to dinner). Even after the discoveries of the great physicist from Switzerland, they managed to keep making time — as if they held a personal, yet collective, grudge against the alpine horologists — and would continue to forge many free moments, helping these then continue to evade the cold and greedy hands of the clock. Unfortunately, this unit had proven to be the most replaceable, as an entire bank of machines were wheeled in, using punch-cards and clicking calculations in order to cross-reference schedules and trajectories, in order to squeeze more time out of the world than this now obsolescent guild could imagine. The Time-Maker machines were terrifying in their quiet and smug efficiency; as if creating more time than Mother Nature had intended, simply to make more drudge work for others.

Serge took another sip of coffee, which had already become lukewarm. The task he was involved with, emblematic of the fate of the factory, made the coffee taste more bitter perhaps. He recalled a meeting with one of the owner's underlings (but an overling to Serge), whose rather sneering face clearly didn't register any of the foreman's rational protests to the radical new plans. Instead, this unfeeling technocrat watched Serge's hands — fluttering around the foreman's immediate person, as he beseechingly made his case — with a look of disgust or horror; as if they were vampire bats, or squids, or some other kind of hideous creature. The expression seemed to be saying, "look here!…you are making your argument primarily with your hands. And this will no longer *do*. Henceforth, all things will be made with *tools*. Hands are now free to be clean, soft, and idle. Don't you see?!" But Serge continued to insist that he could make the numbers all add up to the owner's satisfaction. And yes; *with his hands,* if need be.

Serge rubbed his eyes of the unpleasant memory, and continued his desultory inventory. But he did so with increasing haste, as the morning whistle was imminent, and he felt the need to soon go stand on his usual iron perch, and watch the men and women arrive one last time. And so he flicked through the pages, making small pencil marks here and there, out of a habitual diligence.

These pages were dedicated to the unit charged with *making noise.* Surprisingly perhaps, this group forged their din without much fuss or noise of their own. It was as if they left their racket for the product itself. Those family folk, who lived across the canal from the factory, were happy when news broke that these workers in particular lost their jobs. Little did they know that the new Noise-Maker machines would carve up their sleep far more efficiently than those other conscientious men and women did. Soon it would be slicing its blades through not only their walls, but their eardrums. Most of these employees arrived already deaf, and yet they managed to make a whole menagerie of noises by hand; some really quite beautiful. Moreover, this department always got along famously with the unit tasked with *making trouble.* An unruly lot, who — ironically — turned out to be the most helpful when it came to organizing the factory's annual picnic. This division managed to make a great deal of trouble, however, for the machines which were installed to replace them; to the extent where the contraptions had to be relocated and bolted to the ceiling, where the workers could no longer tamper with them.

Serge looked at the names in the rest of the ledger: those units responsible for *making up* and *making over* — each department with its own special skills, protocols, codes, languages, and gestures. Curiously, the original owner — an affable visionary, who was the grandfather of the younger, and altogether less likeable, man, who was now putting them all out to pasture — did not see any reason to create a unit for *making believe.* He said: "The industrial age has no need of make-believe. Let us leave such things in the age of religion." However, the new boss understood that the modern age still craved such a thing, and always would. As long as it wasn't made by hand. Fantasies forged by machines was the future. He had said at much at a recent share-holders meeting, to great applause. Indeed, such highly engineered flights of fancy were to be largely co-produced by the brand new unit, which was to be unveiled to the press, with great fanfare, when the factory reopens in late Fall. There was much secrecy around this new unit; and Serge had kept his promise, not to tell any of his colleagues. (Although this was more out of distaste and tact, than any loyalty to the company, at this stage in the game.)

Serge shook his head, reading the name of this new department. It seemed cheap to him. It was as if the owner was trying to sell his wares to people who lived inside a talking picture, and not in the real world. Perhaps, if this unit's intangible commodity were hand-made, he could imagine it would make people's lives better. But as it was, having seen the cold and shining chrome of its impersonal source, he was not so sure. Nevertheless, Serge knew deep in his stomach that profits would rapidly rise. How could they not, with so few workers to pay? And now with such limited skills!…milling about the factory floor, hands in their pockets, kicking machines every now and again, when they hiccup oil onto the ground.

Serge tapped the name of this secret new department with the stiff piece of rubber on top of his pencil, as if erasing the words would somehow erase the dismal destiny that had been planned for the factory.

New Unit, #9 — Making Love

But before he could take out his frustration with such a symbolic gesture, the morning whistle blew, and the sounds of human voices flooded into Serge's stranded ark, for the last time at such volume.

THE GESTURE OF DESTROYING

When [disturbance and destruction] are without intention, however, when they occur with "pure motives," then they are evil, which happens rarely because it is inhuman (as is "pure good," regrettably.) And then they are terrifying.
— Flusser, *Gestures*, 60

Some called her Abaddon. She had silver-grey wings with razor edges and yawned a lot and she was very old, though it didn't show. Some called her Amanita. She had been sent down a long time ago to what is now New Jersey to collect the soil that would be used to create Adam. It was kind of fun — exercised her creative impulses, etc. — and so she stayed, and found more soil, and kept going. Except this time she kept the soil for herself, and tried her hand at some of her own heavenly sculpting. She decided that Adam would be less lonely if he had a dog to keep him company, and so she grabbed some dirt and went to work. The first one didn't come out so well, and so she tried again. That one didn't look right, either, and so she took more soil and made a third. After several days of this — and several thousand attempts — Abaddon yawned and realized this wasn't her particular calling. She kept her half-puppies around her for sentiment's sake: later people would refer to them as "locusts" and paint images of the woman surrounded by a sea of tiny dogs with human faces and tiger teeth and what looked like scorpion stingers on their tails. (When she saw some of these images she thought, Come on, they don't look THAT bad...) One afternoon she woke up from a nap and looked over at the dogs and for no reason at all she incinerated all of them.

And so the destroying angel left off from her experiment in sculpting, and she beat her shiny silver-grey wings and moved on to other things. Perhaps I will be a writer, she thought. She bought a laptop and began a novel about her thousands of little mutant puppies, and she invented thousands of worlds for them to inhabit and thousands of lives for them to live, and when she got to the end she printed it all out — it took three days to do so — and built a wall with the pages and perched the computer on top. When it was done she stood back and faced the wall, and yawned, and beat her razored wings until the entire thing was shredded.

Perhaps I will be an orator, she thought. She signed up for voice lessons at the community center, and read the works of Quintillian, and watched old presidential debates on YouTube, and studied the speeches of the speakers she admired. And one morning, after falling asleep while reading Cicero, she woke up and spun her head around and whipped her knife-wings across her own face until nothing of her mouth remained but a bloody hole.

Perhaps I will be a maker of things, she thought. She took on-line courses in woodcraft and the electronic arts, and sent away for parts, and when the parts arrived she tried anew to make those little dogs for Adam — he might not be around to appreciate them anymore, but his descendants sure were — and she built roomsful of tiny breathing robots with dogs' bodies and men's faces and sent them off to make their tiny breathing robot fortunes in the world. (She kept one or two at home for company.) And one day she summoned them all back, having grown lonely, and made tiny little beds for all of them, in which they could rest and recharge. And while they rested, she dispatched roomsful of tiny robot nurses holding tiny pillows to smother each one in its sleep.

Perhaps I will be a lover, she thought.

The Gesture of Destroying

Moira began destroying things before she was born.

While still gestating in her mother's belly, Moira destroyed her mother's figure, complexion, and social life. By the eighth month, she had destroyed her mother's sense of youth and possibility, while also destroying her father's peace of mind, and plans for the future. This previously amiable and easygoing couple had, however, planned for a child. So these particular forms of destruction were absorbed by Moira's parents, who adored each other. It would take more than pregnancy to ruin their marriage, they told each other, through their eyes and fatigued smiles. But even as an embryo, Moira could sense all the things that awaited her in the wider world, beyond the nervous tattoo of her mother's heartbeat: things that would soon turn naive and unblinking faces towards her, not expecting the fearful purity of her strike.

When Moira was born, she permanently destroyed her mother's capacity for intense physical pleasures, just as she destroyed the doctor's eardrums with her preternatural and piercing shrieks. The newborn's skull was abnormally hard and obstinate, launching her into the world like a torpedo, or blunt ice-breaking frigate. The mother's screams matched the child's; although the latter's contained a cold fury that the other's did not.

During her first year of life, Moira destroyed the sleeping patterns of her well-meaning guardians, and with it, their general equilibrium. As a toddler, she destroyed the toys that were brought to her with parental trepidation. She enjoyed the texture of the synthetic hair of her dolls between her teeth, before ripping them out from the roots like a wild animal. She enjoyed pulling the arms off of soft toys, and tearing down the mobile of colorful birds that hung suspended above her crib. Moira's parents feared that she was somehow innately feral. But feral creatures are not evil. They are simply wild. Undomesticated. Moira had a method to her malice, and gained great pleasure from its deliberate and unclouded purpose.

By age ten, Moira's father had rebaptized his daughter — silently, in his own thoughts — Kali. This rather gangly suburban goddess — so unprepossessing at first glance — had indeed, by this stage, succeeded in separating her parents. Once or twice a year, Moira's mother would occasionally meet her ex-husband at a diner downtown for lunch, punctuated by long pickle-flavored pauses, on condition that he not bring "the child" with him. By this stage, this very same child had swiftly destroyed her father's career, which had once been very promising, before this young demon arrived in their lives, with her pockets full of powder kegs.

As a teenager, Moira destroyed the self-esteem of any fellow students who dared to approach her, as well as the teachers who tried to help this problem child, with the dirty blonde hair, and the red-tinted eyes. By this stage, Moira's destructive tendencies were so natural to her, so effortlessly executed and enjoyed, that she didn't necessarily realize she was doing it. By now, there was little intention to her thoughts, words, or actions that could be deemed cruel. Destruction merely followed in her wake, as if she was a Pacific Rim tsunami, reborn in the shape and aspect of an adolescent girl. When, for instance, Moira found herself alone in the high school art room, surrounded by the recently fired clay animals — the ones that her peers had lovingly created with their clumsy, childish hands — she barely even registered that she was being destructive, as she tipped them one by one on to the floor, leaving a crunching blanket of archeological shards for the janitor to sweep up; his head shaking at the Sisyphean senselessness of his vocation.

On occasion, however, Moira would begin to reflect on her destructive nature, and wonder if she was as evil as everyone said she was. "Does evil *feel* evil?" she wrote in her diary, before destroying the book that very same evening; page by page, fed into the fire that she made in the garden. (Despite her natural attraction to fire, Moira felt that arson, when applied to more ambitious projects, was cheating — outsourcing destruction to an element other than herself, and thus robbing her of the right to take most of the credit.) As a young woman, she read about her spiritual ancestors: looters, vandals, barbarians, pirates, pillagers, soldiers, and terrorists. She enjoyed the tales of explorers, and other imperial agents, who brought destruction to new worlds by camel, sail, train, or inside their own sneezes; just as she relished the legacy of bankers, investors, and real estate "developers," who developed only their own images of the future, like film negatives in the sun: bleaching the lives and livelihoods of others into a bright oblivion. Reading about such economic rapine, she felt keenly the difference between a picturesque ruin, and a demolished building: the latter being infinitely more noble and satisfying to her soul. And yet none of these agents of destruction rose to her impeccable standards, since they all put taper to wick for a reason; albeit an unjustifiable one. They all destroyed with an alibi, an excuse, a mission, a calling, a plan, or a signature from the authorities. This belittled their achievements in her eyes, since they were not pure. These were means towards an end, whereas Moira's actions were only a series of ends, each their own unique and uncompromising terminus. Of particular interest to Moira, among these imperfect kindred spirits, were the Luddites, who destroyed machines in order that they themselves could be able to continue their productive work. This paradox confused and troubled her. As did the tales of her pseudo-namesake, Kali. A goddess of destruction, who cleared the cosmic way for rebirth. Was there no hope of a pure destruction, then? No possibility of irredeemable havoc?

As a woman in full bloom, Moira liked to get drunk and tip over chessboards in dark cafés. This occasionally led from astonished and heated words to sexual congress. But her addled sensual companions would soon run scurrying from her bed, clutching their clothes, and counting themselves lucky to have escaped at all. At such moments, flushed and exhilarated, Moira would lie alone in her bed and fantasize about the universe before the Big Bang; its inky void seducing her with its restless absence. The mythic moment would build and build in her mind's eye: nothingness itself, pressing on the window pane of existence, like black snow, forcing itself through a cabin window during an avalanche. And just as the explosion of cosmic matter ignited in her brain and body, she would shudder with conflicted excitement. All that sudden substance, appearing *ex nihilo,* and now awaiting destruction. Destruction wrought through the violent collision of black holes, the spectacular collapse of dark stars, or through the more subtle and exquisite demise of entropy itself. The sheer, pitiless unfolding of inevitability.

At such moments, Moira's consciousness was as sharp and focused as the poisoned tip of Time's Arrow itself. (Zeno be damned!) She respected the universe for destroying everything it creates, eventually. Whether this was God's sinister plan, or some allegorical blind watch-maker, it didn't matter to her. As long as there were broken springs, smashed coils, warped gears, and other delirious detritus strewn all over the floor of this divine workshop. Indeed, Moira wished that she herself possessed the patience and maturity — not to mention the infinite life-span — to watch the universe destroy *itself,* like a snake eating its tail. But she was in fact too addicted to the thrill of destruction to delay her own gratification. She was too habituated to the feeling that the gesture of destroying created within her; distorting her thoughts, her face, her body, her behavior into a kind of fearful grace.

She simply adored being abhorred.

By the time Moira reached middle age, the autumn years beginning to curl their dry and flaky fingers about her, she had stopped thinking about destruction altogether. And yet it continued to trail all about her, like a black wedding train, or dark plumes of blood, blossoming in a warm bath. The lined reflection in her mirror seemed increasingly surprised that she herself was succumbing to entropic forces. By virtue of her own inhuman instincts, she had presumed that she was exempt from mortal, even physical, laws. Had she been seeking freedom all this time, through her destructive gestures? No. That would have been too human; resulting from a banal and pragmatic self-interest. The modes of destroying she now deployed so unthinkingly, like the condensation of breath or the scattering of bird seeds, had nothing in common with the everyday experience of mere disruption or disturbance. (Both of which could be traced back to certain psychic alloys forged between self and world, in the touchingly deluded interests of the former.) That is to say, if Moira had tipped over the chessboard while in the midst of playing the game, then she would no doubt have a reason for doing so: to avoid losing. Such a gesture would have been a perverse form of respect for the rules of the game, and indeed for her opponent. But to disturb the chessboard sitting innocently between two strangers, and disrupt *their* game? This is a very different relationship to one's fellow man, and the gestures they expect, in order to maintain a bare minimum of civilization. Such an act is senseless and anti-social. And therein lies its special tang, for those rare souls who truly put no stock whatsoever in either sense or society.

When Moira died, her own purity of action remained, echoing off all the walls that she had ever touched, and aloof from the usual ambivalent compromises of her kind. Indeed, her own death was a *tour de force,* no less impressive for being imperceptible to the outside world. Every failure of nerve, organ, tissue, and cell was the result of her own will and attention; accumulated over many agonizing, ecstatic months, and turned inward. She did not fight the forces of finitude in her body. Rather she welcomed them, like a lavish and indulgent host. Her system became so reversed that she seemingly breathed in carbon dioxide, and exhaled oxygen, to better fuel explosions of the future. Flowing now into pure stillness, emptied of both perception and intention, she finally destroyed her own stubborn tendency to avoid destruction, leaving only the temporary contours of hollowness itself.

THE GESTURE OF PAINTING

Come here. You'll have to stoop down a bit to fit through the door.

If you look to your left you'll see her. She has blue eyes and her hair is half-shorn, orange in some parts, streaked with purples, other parts left brown indiscriminately. When you look there, notice the brush in her hand. (Look and see that she is missing a finger: she was separated from it in an accident some years ago and had it capped with her old babyhair and fashioned into a brush. Watch as she holds it and the finger once again becomes part of her hand, skin cradling bone.)

She began painting when she was very young, sitting with her grandfather and watching as he ground leaves, seeds, and stones to color his work, made beetle reds and cowpiss yellows and, as he got older, began slowly to burn his things, instead — orange rinds from breakfast, bits of couch cushion, undershirts, scraps of wallpaper — and used the ash and charcoal to cover his canvases. In time he sat naked on cushionless springs among his peeled walls, and he burned more intimate things to make his drawing media — small trinkets given to him by the wife who had passed, Scrabble tiles with which he had built the love letters he wrote to her every night on the board they had used to play together while she was alive, pages of her diaries — and the little girl helped him mix the soot into linseed oil and spread it across the canvases, and the walls, and his face, and the windows, until one afternoon she came to visit and the room was bare and blackened and he had disappeared into it.

There is no charcoal, here. She never paints in grays or blacks. She has instead made pigments of herself, dipping her brush into pots of drying oils mixed with little piles of dry tattooed skin, powdered lacquered nail clippings, shavings of dyed hairs or green-mascaraed eyelashes. She colors herself so as to become the color she paints with.

Look again. But be careful how you look. Watch as she turns to look back at you. As you give her your gaze you, too, become part of her pigment. Look down at your sleeve: wasn't that blue this morning? Pull out your phone and look at your reflection in the screen: were your eyebrows always so thin? When did your lips turn flesh-toned? She has taken your freckles, the tinted lotion you applied this morning. The quickly fading blue of your jeans is soaking into the wall — do you see it?

Look back at her. The walls around her are covered in handprints, in dark and dusty browns (you run your fingers through your hair and feel it turning brittle as the color bleeds out), in powdery whites (your increasingly bloodshot eyes itch as you feel the whites disappearing). Now there are spindly-legged creatures on the wall in ochres and oranges (and your skin is lightening) and you realize she is making a cave painting.

And so, as you begin to feel increasingly transparent you do the only thing you can think of. You turn around, and you look at the door, and you begin to work. Gently you brush your fingers across the wood. She hears the sound and turns to look. And as she does so, your fingertips begin to leave the slightest traces of orange and violet. Your hands move in circles, and as the colors intensify, you move them to your body. She watches as you softly brush aqua across your cheeks, rub greens into your brow and shiver as your fingers graze a translucent onyx throat. She shivers, too, and you go on like this, forgetting yourself until you hear a sigh behind you. You turn to look, and she's no longer there.

But there's a mirror on the far wall, and if you walked to it and looked inside you would see a mandala staring back at you. And you would understand that you're now trapped here — if you stepped back outside the door you would blow away in a thousand colors. Now sit down, painter, and wait for your next visitor.

The Gesture of Painting

Sudeep stared at the ceiling, his eyes tracing every crack in the peeling paint. Lying on top of his sweaty mattress, on the floor, he wondered whether some of the lead flakes break off and fall into his mouth as he slept, like toxic snow. Not that he slept very much these days. The bedroom was completely empty and unadorned, save the mattress; his lethargic body on top of it; and the sunlight which poured through the curtainless window. A year ago, this sunlight felt like a blessing from God. But on this day, it revealed the chilly melancholia, hidden deep within its warming rays.

For Sudeep had lost his lover, to the disease which his beloved Michael had fought so bravely. And now Sudeep found this missed visage among the cracks on the ceiling. Visions of their love, and lovemaking, played across this surface, as if it were a cracked screen; as damaged as the smartphone which lay on the floor next to him, with no missed calls. These memories did not arouse Sudeep, as his heart was far too heavy. But he did, at that moment, recall a confession he once made to one of his friends: that Americans were the best lovers, because they were the most repressed and ashamed. And Michael was nothing if not the all-American boy.

Together they had moved to Detroit, in order to start an idealistic new life together, helping the local community, and filling the enormous house — bought in full, with a surprisingly modest inheritance — with objects both beautiful (from Michael) and kitsch (from Sudeep). But the diagnosis came soon after, and the great gathering of nesting fetishes never occurred. Too much time and money was spent on doctors, tests, medications, palliatives, and distractions. They didn't even get to enjoy the montage moment that all new domestic couples deserve: the painting of the house in fresh coats and colors. Something about the decrepit surfaces around them made sense, as Michael's condition, and his own frame, deteriorated. So they lived among flakes and chips and the honest evidence of Time's indiscriminate tendency to strip bare. A house stripped of laughter and levity. But not stripped of love. Even after Michael's body was no longer to be found. Just a mattress on the floor. Some political magazines in the bathroom. And a coffee machine in the kitchen, almost the size of a small European car.

After a long stretch of such unmoving mourning, Sudeep experienced a mental sea change. He suddenly recalled Michael's love of art, and all the times that they had spent together in the Met, the MoMA, and the Thursday night exhibition openings around Chelsea. Sudeep showered and dressed for the first time in what felt like weeks, finally throwing away the cardboard and plastic remnants of meals ordered to the house, and hardly touched.

He spent two hours in a second-hand bookstore, and brought home as many coffee table books of the great artists as his weakened arms and backpack could carry. He studied the Pantone color catalogue as if it were the Talmud. He researched brushes on the Internet, as if they were nannies he was going to entrust the care of his children to. He took out a loan, and went to the hardware store every day for two months, bringing home can after can of paint — all the colors of the rainbow, and every shade in between — until these were hard to avoid, on the floor, on the stairs, in the bath, and on the kitchen counter. He felt each tin to be a new friend, revealing new vistas and possibilities. They all talked to him, in a voice not unlike Michael's, suggesting modes of inter-chromatic realization. And as he watched the paint shaker machine in the hardware store, Sudeep felt like its violent mechanical shudder was shaking him out of his depression.

Sudeep practiced his latent painting skills (he had attended, and then dropped out of, art school) on one large wall in the living room, until he felt the gesture returning to his body, like an old dance that he had forgotten. His head would cock to the side, his eye would squint, and his elbow would guide. He painted and painted, layer over layer, creating vast palimpsests in different, improvised styles, until the multicolored vision became too heavy to stay affixed to the wall, and came curling and crashing down: a giant wave of paint, thudding on to the floor, which he then rolled out like a carpet, and carried into the garden.

Sudeep paid the postman, a middle-aged Ukrainian with ample curves, to model for him, in order to practice and refine his facility with faces and figures. The postman blushed to begin with, but was clearly flattered to be the object of such an intense gaze, and almost sacred process of replication. For his part, Sudeep was always amazed that the brush — which seemed so inert and innocuous, when standing in a mason jar — would complete a circuit, and become part of not only his body, but the wider assemblage of elements: model, image, imagination, weather, mood…capture. Through this wooden finger — both blunt and exquisite — Sudeep pointed to a more hopeful future, even as his every gesture was a form of fidelity to the past.

This crumbling mansion had eight rooms, and so the master of the house narrowed down his styles — one for each room. The giant living space would be the Bosch room, since it pleased his sense of irony that a living room would be filled with macabre and morbid figures heralding finitude. And so he painted his own Garden of Earthly Delights, all around the fireplace, and up to the fake chandelier; each imp with the face of a previous acquaintance or enemy (depending on the situation these figures found themselves). This initial masterpiece took longer than expected, so Sudeep invited a neighbor to help him, during one of his tea breaks on the front stairs. Aeshe was a serious young girl of twelve, with cornrows and spectacles, through which she peered at the world with a laconic suspicion. But when she saw what Sudeep had already achieved in the Bosch Room, she agreed to be a part of his project. And so she helped with the Van Gough room; that is, the main bedroom. And soon the walls were no longer off-cream and peeling, but vibrant and pulsating with gorgeous sunflowers and starry nights.

Aeshe brought in some friends from around the neighborhood to help with the Kandinsky room, which appealed to their child-like imaginations. As did the Pollock room, of course, which Sudeep outsourced to the kids completely. (Truth be told, he found it just as therapeutic to watch these young souls and bodies hurling paint at the walls, and getting splashed in the process, as doing it himself.) He laughed with them, even as the longer they worked, the more they became involved in the gestures rendered in scatters and spatters. At one point, Sudeep even had to intervene, to stop a budding argument around aesthetics; gently explaining to Jerome — an overweight boy with a tendency to wheeze — that sometimes form *is* content.

Even more cathartic, though incredibly intricate, was the Caravaggio room, which Sudeep reclaimed for his solitary vigil. He had trouble capturing the light of the master, and knew that he would never climb to the heights of his Pantheon, but rather present an homage to their spirits; like those folk-made posters for Hollywood films in Zambia, that bring their own idiosyncratic energy to a more established style.

After finishing the Turner room, and the Klimt salon, Sudeep took a two-week holiday, camping in Alaska, to clear his mind and palette. His dreams all had the texture of canvas. The inside of his eye-lids were leafed in gold on one side, and watercolors on the other. And he knew he had to flush all those shades away, to tackle his last room. A project he both craved and dreaded.

So he returned refreshed, with the smell of mountains and wind in his prematurely greying hair. He selected his brush, as if selecting a companion to go on a long journey with. Took a deep breath, in front of a completely white wall. Opened a tin of black paint. As black as death. And began mixing it with paint the color of blood; the blood that too often escaped his lover's body. It was time to begin the Rothko room.

The Gesture of Photographing

She was born eyeless but with a kind of sight in her fingers, her cameras, her takers of touch and outline and her little spinners of apparition. She saw in moments that connected themselves or not, and so she lived sometimes frame by frame and sometimes in a sequence of small pannings across and back and then again. As she grew her fingertips shed themselves like snakeskin and new patterns grew in their place, new perspectives and new forms of truth and new illusions and new trickery. She kept a box of her fingerprints, and when she picked them up and pressed them to her lips they let her see again in the ways she had when she was younger.

One finger saw the way birds see, draping surfaces with more color than she knew how to understand or share. (This was a lonely kind of sight.)

One finger saw like a frog.

One finger saw like an octopus, touching the colors of things into being.

One finger was a kaleidoscope, briefly and sweetly, during a great and consuming love.

One finger only saw in the light and night of an erupting volcano, reds and oranges and smoke.

One finger saw underwater.

One finger saw like a snake, in waves and pulses of the heat coming off bodies as they moved.

One finger saw the world in slow motion, like a dragonfly.

(She had once dipped a fingertip into a glass of gin and from then on it spun and whirled the vision that it gave her.)

One finger was for a wide-eyed taking of the world, like a child takes.

One finger saw the world as if lying down and looking up through its canopy.

One finger was only for recognizing faces.

One finger could see constellations in the daytime.

She was careful to wear gloves in company. (If she stroked a finger across your skin, she would give you visions. If she used two fingers, she would send you into ecstasy…but only for a moment. Three fingers had driven people mad. Once she touched a lover with all of her fingertips, very softly and very carefully and very very slowly, one at a time.)

(She had only done that once.)

As she picked her way through the box of fingerprints — the box of photographs — she took each one out and carefully taped it to the wall. By the time the box was empty she had used up her tape and the wall was covered in ridges, a map of forms of vision, a map of herself, and she gently brushed her lips across them, one by one, and tasted the worlds of her past. And after she had spent some time this way, she chose from among them, and plucked them off the wall, and put them in her bag, and went to sleep.

The next day she left the room and walked down the street with her bag of fingerprints to visit a tattoo artist she knew. It took a day and a night and by the time they had finished she left his studio and returned home covered in fingerprints. She spent a week, and then another, alone and still and healing.

And then one evening she made a call, and the doorbell rang, and she opened the door, and she reached out one fingertip (this was a finger that saw like a prism) until she felt the bridge of a nose, and a cheek, and a chin, and she used that finger to hook the collar of the shirt of the man attached to these parts, and she drew him inside and shut the door behind them. (If you could see him, you would notice that he was also born without eyes. And if you had visited his home, you would also find a box of tactile whorled and ridged prints from his own life seeing with fingertips. He had never shown her that box.)

And so he readies his lips, and the photographer — her body now covered in her work — prepares for her first exhibition.

The Gesture of Photographing

Mr. D. felt himself the dense focal point of the dark room in which he had not left for more than three weeks. His lungs were filled with fluid, just as his soul was heavy with fatigue. There was a sharp pain which accompanied each shallow breath, just below his left shoulder blade, which insinuated itself as a kind of swallowed, stubborn second pulse, measuring the seemingly interminable passage of his illness. The thick velvet curtains protected him from almost all external light, even though the clock was conscientiously ticking itself just past noon, and a gas lamp hissed near his bedside, should he gather the strength to read. (Something which happened only for minutes at a time, if at all, on some days.) The patient both welcomed and dreaded the almost hourly appearance of his solicitous sister, who would fluff his pillows, and bring him tea, broth, medicine, soporifics, and news from the outside world — whether it be of the village, or the wider world.

Mr. D. was dying. He could feel it. Slithering through his fleshly vessel like a thousand tiny black serpents, breeding and hatching the end of all tomorrows. And yet he did not feel the dread he expected. He trusted in God to receive him; despite his sins and faults, having spent his later years repenting, scrubbing his thoughts with strict mental hygiene, and collecting an accumulation of banal but surely effective good graces. As he stared at the ceiling — a dark blue, featureless landscape which had become the very shade and texture of his monotonous consciousness since falling ill — the gas lamp sputtered and died. Mr. D. had no breath to call for assistance; and so he stared into the sudden darkness, half-wondering if he had indeed just died. Slowly, however, a few rays pushed their way past the velvet curtains and wormed their way into his retinas; and the sounds of passing horses persisted in cantering across his eardrums. It appeared to the patient that he hadn't been snuffed out just yet.

Indeed, the sudden darkness soothed him, and he felt as free from troublesome thoughts or prickled emotions as the unseen, but intimately felt, furniture in the room. Suddenly, however, as his eyes adjusted, a vision emerged out of the void, and imprinted itself on the ceiling above him. It was a colorful carbon copy of the small church across the road; inverted. For a moment, once again, Mr. D's rather uncertain mind took this as a sign from his Maker. But the patient was sufficiently a gentleman of his era that he soon guessed at the scientific reasons for this unexpected spectral visitation. By virtue of accidental physics, the bedroom was acting as a *camera obscura,* thanks to the absence of the gaslight, and the sun's rays, which were now — thanks to organic optics — sending him a natural photograph of the world outside. The somewhat watery image — rusty colored stone, and the delicate green of the ivy wrapped around the spire — were exquisite to the invalid, who had been staring at a featureless, flat canopy for weeks. It was a delicate thing of beauty.

Occasionally the floating photograph would shift into motion, like a magic lantern, as when a slight breeze obliged the ivy leaves to rustle in little wavelets; or when a carriage went by, revealing only a trio of top hats and a single ivory-colored parasol, extending down from the top of the "frame." Mr. D. felt unexpected tears pricking his eyes, and the image became blurry. He was entranced by this spontaneous window on to an upside-down world; a world that he was surely departing soon.

Here was a souvenir to travel to the next life with, in the front pocket of his memory.

Indeed, the rather tranquil and Spartan room of his mind was suddenly jolted, as if an overstuffed suitcase, that he had placed on top of a wardrobe in a deliberate act of planned negligence, had finally toppled from its perch, and come crashing the ground, flinging its forgotten contents to every corner of his soul.

One specific memory rose up to him, as vivid as the little church scene, superimposing itself upon it. He was standing in the garden of the L. family; seized in the fierce pincers of both anger and misery. He was facing away from the house that he had been trying to summon signs of life from, for many minutes. The sun was setting, and he distinctly recalled the wheelbarrow propped up against the wall, as well as the intricate Oriental bells that hung from the lime-tree (one of his many offerings to this domestic clan). The family had clearly fled in relative haste, as the house had not been "turned down" for the off-season. He sensed once again in his bones, reliving the humiliation, that he was likely the spur for this sudden, and untimely migration back to the city. But it had been a misunderstanding! *A misunderstanding, I tell you!* And yet, no matter how many letters he would subsequently write, explaining the size, shape, provenance, and dire repercussions of this misunderstanding, the only reply he ever received came in the form of a very deliberate silence, monogrammed with the L. family seal.

Peeling loose from the present, Mr. D. felt himself traveling to the same place, there in the warm garden, with thunder rumbling and a blustery breeze pawing the treetops of the valley, even as he was still stricken to his bed. His skin was etched with papery creases, this time, and his hair was shot with grey. But there he was. Again. As before. Abandoned.

And yet, on this occasion the bitterness had lost its poison. Indeed, he could not taste it at all. The projections continued, originating deep in his being, spooled across his memory, and shimmering out into the room; as if his entire life was now a *camera obscura,* and his every breath a gaseous glass plate that bore a message of release. He saw the young girl, A., posing for him, in the same garden, since his magic machine required the long exposure of the outdoors. He heard her sisters making gentle fun of the hasty, musty and old-fashioned props that he assembled around the young sylph. He felt her parents watching with some concern from the conservatory; but reassuring each other, more with subtle elisions and tea-spooning gestures than actual words, that a man of the cloth could have no unsavory motives. He had assured them that this device neither stole nor entrapped souls, but rather captured the essence of its subject, only to return it tenfold, through the miracle of motherless reproduction. Did they themselves fear for their souls when sitting for an oil painting? Well, then! This is no different. Indeed, there is less cause for misgivings, as the process is much faster, and clearly occurs with God's blessing, since it happens with little or no human intervention. One would spend one's time more wisely admonishing the stones for remembering the shells, leaves, or fish that persist in the fossil.

Indeed, at times Mr. D. felt more like a gardener than that strange new creature, the gentleman photographer. He would push the sturdy wooden legs of his camera into the soft ground, and then he would plant seeds. Soon enough, photographs would bloom. It was still unclear to him whether he was engaged in an art, science, craft, or technique. Either way, he felt more continuity with the practices of his forebears than rupture. After all, weren't the trees themselves photosynthesizing? Isn't the sun itself a flashing device, with an inordinately long exposure? Aren't our fellow men and women sensitive plates of a sort, registering the specificity of light at any given moment, and storing each layer in their hearts. A type of animation. Was not God the ultimate photographer, staging and memorializing every moment on this earth? From this perspective, Mr. D. himself was merely paying homage to the grace of holy sight and sacred insight. "Let there be light."

And let there be things to write of, in the divine medium of light.

Such were the inchoate philosophies that Mr. D. had starting developing in a little treatise, that he had dedicated and given to the L. family, in order that they might better understand his quiet and unusual passion for recording their lives. Here he had explained, with a Deacon's modest mastery of rhetoric, that there was little difference whether the subject was the household fruit bowl, pet dog, or daughter. These all were aspects of God's plan, each with their place and purpose, for which the machine would capture but one fleeting moment, to enable reflection and gratitude. "The man with the apparatus is not hunting for reflected light," he had written in his portable notebook, while drafting his treatise, "but rather selecting specific rays of light within the parameters of those available to him." Everything upon which Mr. D. turned his glassy third eye towards responded to being watched, whether it was the youngest maiden of the house, or the horses in the fields. Even the pond, empty of all visible life shimmered differently, under the passage of the water-striders. Every exposure was a portrait. Even a landscape. So that giggling girls and silent trees were equally self-conscious under his mnemonic gaze. (A phrase which he borrowed for the title of his little book on the subject.) This new way of seeing — a way of seeing which fixes what is seen — encourages an appreciation for singularity, he insisted. It selects *this* tree, from *this* angle, at *this* moment. And through the very framing of the unique, it creates one piece in a never-to-be-completed collage called the Eternal.

But such high-sounding words soured on the page, after the Misunderstanding. Indeed, the book itself had served as a missile thrown at Mr. D.'s person on that unfortunate afternoon, the hard-leather corner catching him on the cheek, and leaving a bruise. A. herself had vanished upstairs during the commotion, and that was the last time he had seen her in person. Thankfully Mr. D. still had her image, imprinted on paper. But he half-suspected even these traces would evaporate soon enough, by virtue of her ongoing absence. (Did she forgive him? Did she miss him? Did she understand him?…He would never know.)

After this incident, he continued to refine his photographic praxis. But it never felt quite so devout again; no longer tied to a greater mission. Indeed, at times he wondered if he was in fact fingerprinting the world, as one takes the fingerprints of a criminal: a thought that led him to abandon the whole enterprise years before he found himself, unable to get out of bed, indeed, unable to cling much longer to his own vitality.

He realized now the hubris of his former years, and how much time he had spent upon it. The gentleman photographer thought he had been doing God's work, but was instead naively attempting to *play* God. In posing his young muse just so, he was attempting to precisely capture the enigmatic intersection of time and space. But these two coiling lines will forever escape the mortal desire to fix their secret congress. The image which remains is merely a caricatured phantom of what is. Or what was.

The true camera is the one we stumble upon, or find ourselves within, like this room in the North end of town, with the creaking pipes along the walls. We are forever inside the mechanism, and should understand ourselves as the subjects of its gaze; and not the master observer. Moreover, "writing in light" is not at all about preserving the past, or being haunted by what was (despite both popular and expert opinion). Rather, it is about fashioning steps upon which we can more mindfully walk towards the future. Had he the time, energy, and materials to revisit his treatise on the subject, Mr. D. would have emphasized this unacknowledged aspect of the art, with its forward-looking orientation. Indeed, had he himself fully appreciated that the gesture of photographing permits us to see, concretely, how choice functions as a projection into the future, then he may not have forsaken the practice, which had become for him mildewed with melancholy.

Indeed, as Mr. D.'s vision began to blur and withdraw, an eternal moment of great lucidity visited him. The eyes in our heads are cameras, he realized, with no film upon which to print what it sees, save for the dubious medium — the unfaithful clay — of memory. Our fellow creatures are the living images, written in light. Were it not for the sun, we would be virtual whispers of being, blindly groping about in shadows, pressed against the walls of a glass darkly. But with God's grace, the sons and daughters of Adam — our intimates especially — provide pinhole perspectives on the universe. And it is up to us to appreciate that specific illumination of the whole, via our own fleeting flames. The ancients believed that every object had a phantom film, that would fling itself, layer by layer towards the human eye, in order to be seen as such. And as always, the ancients were not far wrong.

And the rusty vision of the church persisted on the ceiling, even as it faded in Mr. D.'s pupils, until he saw nothing. Heard nothing. Felt nothing.

But still, the living photograph on the ceiling persisted, shimmering in the afternoon breeze, until his sister entered the room mid-sentence, throwing open the curtains and inadvertently banishing the picture she was never privileged to see; instead finding her brother in the state she had dreaded for weeks.

THE GESTURE OF FILMING

The miners went into the rock, as they did every morning. They moved their table to the cut in the rock they'd made the day before, and they set chairs around table, and poured coffee from thermoses, and stood, and sipped, and each chose a word (one chose "grapes" and one chose "flute" and one chose "vine" and one chose "kiss"). And when they'd finished their coffee they set cups on table and selves in seats and two became speakers and two became listeners and then they began. The cave was filled with strips of sound. …viiiiiiiiiiiiiiiiiiiiiiiinnnnnnnnnnnnnnnnnnnnnnnnne… …kissssssssssssssssssssssssssssss…

And it went that way for most of an hour, with speakers speaking and the listeners listening. (They sometimes spent whole days this way, mornings given to sounds made and taken, breaks given and roles switched, and stopping for lunch, and coming back, and hollowing out more rock, and heading home for dinner.)

And it went that way for most of an hour, until a listener began to hear speed (viiiiiiiiiiiiiiiiiiiiiiiiiiiiiiiiiiiiiiiiine viiiiiiiiiiiiiine vine vine vinevinevinevinevinevinevivivivivivivivivivivivi) and he looked at the fastmoving lips of the speaker and stopped and

85

stood and so did the rest and they looked at the rock of the wall above the viney strip of sound and they saw the surface come alive with dark images — a flexing of shadow shoulders barnacled with sea shells, a smacking-together of wet-bearded shadow lips. One took a sheet of very thin glass from a box on the floor, and he passed it to another, who placed the sheet against the wall and traced the shadows with his stylus. The miner traced until the shadows shifted, and he placed the finished sheet on the floor, and he took another, and he did it again. The four passed the morning this way, until the sheets were stacked tall and the shadows had lifted.

When that was done, they stood to the side and they watched as the stack of glass began to sweat droplets. They turned from the glass to attend to themselves and the first looked down to see his stylus turned trident, and the second tasted a mouthful of salt, and the third heard the sound of a conch shell being blown, and the fourth went blind as his eyes turned to pearls, and the first three looked at the last sheet of glass to find shadows playing upon it in the form of a sea god.

The archivist stood by, awaiting the men as they walked from the cave with that last sheet of glass in hand. She took the sheet and said prayers for the god — its moment of birth was its moment of death, the cave a womb and a tomb — and she walked with the sheet down a path in the cave that went far underground. She came at last to the library. There the god stayed — the glass his body his shroud his bones his flesh his power his breath his cry his story his story's decay — until that night the people gathered and took out the sheet and projected its shadows onto the wall. And in this way, they worshipped him. And in this way, they mourned him. And after that, they filed his sheet away.

The next day, the miners went into the rock, as they did every morning, and they moved their table to the cut in the rock they'd made the day before, and they poured coffee, and each chose a word to mark and remember what had come before.

The one who could still hear the sounds of the water chose "conch."

And the one who still traced the shadows in his mind's eye chose "trident."

And the one who could still taste seawater on his lips chose "salt."

And the still-blind one chose "pearl."

And when they had finished their coffee the speakers spoke and the listeners listened. And the cave was filled with strips of sound.

And they stayed that way through the morning, until one of the listeners began to hear reversal (saaaaaaaaalllllltttttttttttttttttttttlll-laaaaaaaalalalalasasasasasasasasasasaaaaaaaaaltasaltalsalatasasasa-sa) and he looked at the twisting lips of the speaker and looked at the rock that was moving with shadows — the plumping of a crown of clouds, the arcing of a bolt of fingers — and the miners fell silent, and the cave grew cold, and one reached for the shivering glass, and they prepared themselves to bear witness to a new storm god in its birth and in its death.

THE GESTURE OF FILMING

Until that very moment, Gaspar had never really noticed the world. This, despite the fact that he was making steady progress into his third decade of inhabiting it. Indeed, this young man remembered the exact moment everything changed, as if it were a film still, pinned somewhere prominent in the velvet lobby of his mind. He was sitting on the side of his creaky bed, holding the letter from his aunt, his hand shaking. His brow sprouted sudden beads of sweat, despite the late autumn weather.

"Dear Gaspar," it began, in the faultless handwriting of his aunt. "You will no doubt find this letter rather odd, coming out of the blue like this, given that we have not seen each other, nor even corresponded, for many years — not since that Easter we spent by the lake. You were just a child then, so I imagine you have changed more than a little. I feel like I know quite a lot about you, however. More than perhaps I should. Which is why I am writing you now." Gaspar's eyebrows had knitted together with curiosity at this point. "You see, I had a dream about you last night. And not just any dream. This one was very vivid. A 'lucid' dream, I suppose they call it. As if I were actually there with you. But more than this, in fact. It was as if I *were* you. Do you see? It was as if I were seeing the world from your eyes."

Here, Gaspar had sat down, intrigued by his (clearly) eccentric aunt, diving into this tale of her strange dream life without any of the usual arabesques of politesse that he and his compatriots would not usually forsake (the equivalent of offering a meal without a sauce). "The details were not exceptional, but they were crystal clear. My dream-self found you in the Tuileries, reading a newspaper. You were particularly taken with a review of the play that you attended the night before, but were too distracted to follow. You were heartened to read that you did not miss anything special. Then I — that is, *you* — drank some coffee and discussed the developing situation in Germany with the old man sitting at the table next to you, for a good ten minutes. You then walked down the Rue de la Castiglione, where you stopped by a window to take note of a dress that you thought would suit your mistress, before sending a telegram to your publisher, noting once again that your modest advance has not yet arrived."

By this time, upon his first reading of the letter, Gaspar's throat had closed up, as if parched beyond all hope of repair. These events had indeed happened to him the previous Monday, four days earlier. And in that very order! His rational mind checked for the date, but it was not a time for social jests or practical jokes. From what he could remember of his Aunt Marie, she was not one to make light of any situation whatever, let alone others. What could be the meaning of it all? Had she arranged for a private detective to follow him, and write down his movements? But for what possible purpose? And how could such a hypothetical person know his thoughts and motivations from distanced observation? The whole thing was as preposterous as it was uncanny. Unfortunately, it was also undeniable.

Aunt Marie's letter had finished on a lighter note, by asking Gaspar to forgive her for sharing such a commonplace dream out of the blue like this. However, since it did indeed involve his person so intimately, she thought he might find it amusing: the fact that she had "borrowed" him for the night, as it were. Moreover, she promised to return the favor, should he be interested in a holiday from his own unique perspective on things, one of these nights.

Gaspar had postponed replying to his aunt until he could find a rational explanation for it. But after consulting with a close friend, and one of his ex-tutors, he was no closer to solving the mystery. And so with a strange inky feeling in his heart, he wrote a letter to his aunt, confessing that she had indeed stowed away in one of his recent experiences, and that they must have some kind of supernatural — or paranormal — sympathetic connections. Gaspar was a young man living not long after the Great War, however. All those tales of spirit mediums and animal magnetism had evaporated, along with the Victorian belief in unbroken moral progress. Nevertheless, there was no denying the phenomenon, even if the forces behind it were, for the moment at least, proving so elusive.

Aunt Marie's response came quickly; her handwriting not nearly as assured and careful as before. "You can't possibly mean this, Gaspar!" it began, as if they had been in the middle of a heated discussion already. "You would not make fun of your poor aunt, would you? Nothing can be gained from that!" But soon she was convinced of her nephew's sincerity — along with his perplexity, now shared equally between them. Moreover, her dreams continued; almost every night. She would write letters providing details, and he would verify them, his sense of reality becoming less and less certain each time. It appeared that she would experience a seemingly random hour from Gaspar's day — sometimes in the morning, sometimes in the afternoon, other times at night — approximately four days after they occurred. Each time she could describe these experiences down to the most minute detail: the precise type of cufflink, the sound of the rain on top of the taxi, the slight pain in the left molar, the dessert that he had abandoned after two bites.

Gaspar and Marie (which is what they called each other, given their new-found intimacy) switched to the telephone to conduct their now daily conversation; their initial sense of disorientation and panic diminishing over time, even as their acute confusion remained. After a while, soothed by each other's voices and mutual predicament, the mystery became an intimate connection that they began to have difficulty imagining living without. Certainly, Gaspar had at first felt rather indignant and violated by this unexpected intrusion into his existence. But he was careful never to blame his aunt directly, but rather whichever Cartesian demon was playing such wicked tricks on the two of them. After all, could he even bathe in privacy anymore? What of his relationship with women? Was he to suspend his romantic life, lest Marie became an unwilling — but no doubt intrigued — voyeur? Or even co-conspirator?

Indeed, an increasing portion of their telephonic discussions became informal analysis of Gaspar's life, complete with advice from Marie, from everything to clothing to diet to the ways of love. As their relationship continued to intertwine — to the extent that Marie was herself Gaspar at least $^1/_{24}$th of the time — *he* also started to dream both of, and as, his aunt. However, these were not glimpses of a recent experience, but rather a selection of moments from her years during the war, and before. (Who exactly was doing the selecting remained a mystery.) As a result, Gaspar's closed nocturnal eyes were opened to new unimagined vistas, as he walked the world as this attractive, strong-willed woman, who seemed to know how to make doors open, and things happen, in ways he did not. He experienced the war as an adult, rather than as a child, albeit in small oneiric glimpses, for Marie had been a volunteer nurse at the Somme. But this was enough for him to know he was very fortunate not to have been a soldier then. The memories were so horrifying and vivid that he had trouble sleeping for weeks. But when he did manage to drift off, he would find another of Marie's memories waiting for him; some more pleasant than others. The merciful shade of a parasol during a trip to Cairo. The dispiriting wine jellies gifted by a halfhearted paramour in London. And the exquisite sensations provided by a gentleman speaking a rustic Italian.

After a while, Marie complained of the monotony of Gaspar's days. And he could not help but agree, after witnessing her own life. Certainly, he was now able to dine on the fruits of a rich lifetime of experiences; but she was trapped in the rather mundane routine of a still undiscovered Parisian writer. It was this moment when Gaspar *really* began to notice the world, since he was living for two now. And all the things he encountered, via his five senses, were for both he and Marie. He wanted to make every moment count. He wanted every minute to be captivating, or thrilling, or amusing, or moving, in case any given experience would be part of Maria's dream later that week. On one occasion, she complained that he had gone to see a moving picture, but the dream had ended before the credits rolled. He had thus been obliged to narrate the rest of the film over the telephone.

Indeed, this exchange was decisive, and radically changed the relationship he had with himself, and his own life, thanks to this strange new entangled chapter in his life. "Perhaps I am some kind of camera," he hypothesized to himself. "One that can also project, like a human magic lantern." In this scenario, Marie's slumbering mind was a screen on which he somehow tele-projected the moving pictures of his existence. This possibility illuminated his soul like a bulb inside an Edison projector, and the mystery itself retreated from their thoughts and conversations, as Gaspar and Marie became increasingly involved in what they called "the mechanics of the thing." *Why* it was happening became less and less important. And in truth, they both began to worry — perhaps only unconsciously — that if they figured out the reason for it, the entire apparatus linking them would break down, and they would have to go back to their isolated existences.

Gaspar began to neglect his writing, and think of himself more as an *auteur* in the new art of the cinema. His two eyes were twin cameras, and the cellular matter of his brain was the celluloid on which he recorded the world. The projection mechanism remained opaque and unlocated, but it seemed to function without any conscious effort, as Marie received his "signals" as clear as crystal, even when she traveled to the Volga for a spa treatment. (They had decided early on not to meet in person, lest the "connection" collapse through proximity.) And so Gaspar would spend many days in the parks, when the weather was fine, seemingly sketching his fellow men and women, but in fact making storyboards for his next "featurette." He found that through meditation before bed, he could "edit" the events of the day in precise and creative ways, making his world far more interesting that it would normally be. He read technical manuals about the cinema, and philosophical treatises as well, trying to improve his art: Gorky, Epstein, Krakauer. He consulted the archives of Marey, and wrote to the Muybridge estate in England. An agent of the latter answered his questions with the minimum of patience and detail, presuming Gaspar to be yet another amateur director, with an eye on Hollywood, given his questions about "pacing…juxtaposition…meaning," and so on. An enigmatic man with a Czech accent, whom he had struck up a conversation in a café, told him: "Film is the first code in which surfaces move, a discourse of photographs." Gaspar had scribbled this down, nodding his head in wine-soaked enthusiasm, but was not sure how this observation could help him upon re-reading with a clear head.

Thus, at any given moment of Gaspar's day, he considered the "rushes" of his film for Marie, to be premiered in a private night screening four days hence. He created an entire system in his mind, to signal to himself where a cut should happen, and where a splice would work best. He also exploited the Kuleshov effect, focusing on a banana peel on the street, and cutting suddenly to a pompous and arrogant man, stepping out of his house. Marie would smile in her sleep before anything had even occurred, and before gravity had had its revenge. Gaspar found himself anxiously awaiting her calls — always at ten past ten in the morning, after breakfast and note-taking — which increasingly began to sound like the quickly dictated cinema reviews journalist-critics make to their newspaper editors over the phone, in order to make it in time for the morning edition.

For her part, Marie found that she too could edit her memories, if she dedicated an hour to doing so, before retiring properly to bed. (For whatever reason, ginger tea seemed to make things cut together all the more smoothly; whereas for Gaspar, it was black olives that made a noticeable difference.) She would lie on her divan next to a table lamp muted by one of her scarves over the shade, and enjoy the chemical sensation of spooling memories over mind sprockets so that her already adventurous life began to yield the sweet pathos lying latent within. With the benefit of her wise hindsight, she created masterpieces which shook Gaspar to the core, until he began to lose confidence in his own cinematic peccadillos. He began to become insanely jealous of lovers she had entertained a quarter of a century earlier; and deliberately cultivate insomnia to avoid not only seeing, but being ravished by, his rivals. This was too much for the young man to bear!…A kind of schizophrenia began to take hold, as he oscillated between man and woman, the present and the past, and his own "films" became increasingly troubled, fractured, incoherent, and "avant-garde."

Marie watched on in distress, and tried to reassure him over the phone, even as she kept him at arm's length, knowing his passion for her was not something real, but a dark fruit of their oneiric entanglement. She tried to edit her memories to soothe and delight him, but he then fumed that he was receiving only censored material, and that he was not to be protected like a child. Moreover, his films were becoming obscene, as he frequented with prostitutes to punish his aunt, who dreamed these experiences as Gaspar, and thus could feel his intense loneliness and frustration.

And so she convinced him to finally meet her in person. And they took hot chocolate in the park, and found it almost impossible to find words. Instead Gaspar would pretend not to be weeping, and Marie would try to hold his hand in quiet concern. After that day, the "screenings" stopped suddenly, and they no longer had direct access to each other's lives — just as they suspected.

For a while they spoke on the phone, but these conversations were stilted, and heavy with silent accusation (though Gaspar would have difficulty articulating his resentment, since his aunt had done nothing wrong, other than live a full and rich life). Time passed, and their dreams returned to the kind of everyday folk. As he matured, Gaspar became increasingly ashamed of his youthful spleen, and resolved to redeem himself in his aunt's now wrinkled eyes. He ate olives with every meal, even breakfast, as he storyboarded the most wonderful tale: based on his own life, but infinitely more rewarding. He traveled to different parts of the country, location scouting. He cast an actress — the sister of a friend — to "play" his aunt, so that he would have someone to confess his stupidity and shame to; along with his desire for her forgiveness. This effort began to consume him, as he edited and reedited everything in his mind, never happy with the final cut. Moreover, Gaspar was terrified that he could not project his masterpiece to Marie, so that these images would simply exist in his own mind: playing over and over for an empty theater.

Occasionally Marie would sense projections in her sleep, but never to the extent where she saw the world from Gaspar's eyes again. He wrote long letters, explaining his efforts, complete with all his storyboards, to which she wrote reassuring responses, assuring him that she could appreciate his great contribution from his production notes, and did not need to see the final result to absolve his youthful passions.

But Gaspar continued to watch, and work — cutting and splicing everything in his mind — until he became weak. In the hospital, he had the inspiration to incorporate the nurse, as a temporal echo of Marie's volunteer service during the war. But this was his last inspiration, before he succumbed to exhaustion.

Gaspar died the night before the next war was declared. As the church bells rang in the night, a film passed over his eyes. And he saw no more.

THE GESTURE OF
TURNING A MASK AROUND

Late summer was the recycling time.

They woke in the morning, smiling, and spent their hours doing whatever it was they typically did, and in the evening they leaned against walls or chairs or doors and they fell smilingly asleep. While they slept, the man came, visiting them one by one.

(Don't fall asleep, the young ones sometimes whispered to each other. If you stay awake, the man can't find you. But they always drifted, and he always came.)

First he took the feet, paper toes clad in paper shoes.

And they sleepily balanced on the stumps of legs, and they smiled at the man as he softly undid the feet from the shoes and laid them flat, one atop the other, in his briefcase.

Next the lower legs, from shin to ankle.

And they wobbled on their knees, and they smiled at the man as he placed these parts of limbs atop the others, arranging them carefully in his case.

Then they lost their upper legs. And their hands. And their forearms, and elbows, and shoulders.

As he lay them on their backs, still they smiled up at the man. He made sure not to wrinkle or rip the bodies as he disassembled them, putting aside the parts that came to him creased or folded. (He would deal with those later.)

As he gently separated necks from torsos, disarticulating bellies from chests, he would look back to find them smiling.

Finally, he came to the heads.

He reached down and unhooked paper straps from paper ears, untied paper ribbons, gently loosened paper buttons from paper lips, and one by one he pulled off the smiling faces. Underneath the faces were the masks.

Some were demonic hannyas, folded from thin paper pressed from hinoki cypress, and covered in glue and crushed seashells. Some were long-beaked doctors, smelling of roses and beetles and camphor. Some were silent dark morettas, woven of paper made from soft black silk and eyelashes. He found masks of paper made from banana leaves, and grasshopper wings, and gold flake, and bamboo, and skin. Tiny smooth ones and wrinkled old ones.

And one by one he took them off.

And he turned them around.

And he looked inside.

And he lifted the masks.

And he placed them over the place his face should have been.

And just for a few seconds, he became a demon, or a queen, or a god, or a clown, or a very bad man, or a very good one.

And each time he took the mask off again, and he folded it flat, and placed it in his briefcase, and closed the case, and locked it shut.

When he got home, the faceless man unlatched his case and gently stacked the paper in piles of parts: legs, and faces, and hands, and the rest. (The masks he put aside.) And then he went to sleep.

When he woke the next day, the man gathered the piles of paper parts and tied them all together with a thick ribbon, and after breakfast he went out with his package. All afternoon he drove, until he came to the tallest point that he could find and got out of his car. He unbound the stack of paper parts, waited for a powerful gust, opened his arms, and thrust the broken bodies into the sky.

As they caught the wind, legs found torsos found arms found hands found faces, and soon the ground was scattered with new paper people. As they learned their articulations and tested their jointings, slowly the puppets got up from the earth, looked to see the other smiling faces around them, and made themselves a world. (Always, they were smiling.)

The man without a face got back in his car and returned home. After he arrived, he opened his briefcase and gently lifted the pile of paper masks he had left there. (The new people would slowly grow new masks of their own, and those would stay hidden until he harvested them in the next recycling.) He carried the pile to his kitchen, retrieved a pair of scissors and some tape from a drawer, took the first mask off the pile, cut out one of the eyes, and taped it to himself. And then he took the second mask, and did the same thing with another eye. As he worked his way down the pile, the place where his face should have been gradually became a patchwork of chins and nostrils, moustaches and dimples, and too many lips and eyebrows where they should not have been. When he was done, he walked to the bathroom and looked in the mirror out of the eye of a demon and the eye of a clown. As the taped paper parts sank into his skin and rearranged themselves into a horrible beautiful symmetry, he found himself satisfied with what he saw. And so the man walked to his bedroom, and turned off the lights, and went to sleep for another year, now that he could smell and taste and feel and see his dreams again. And when his paper sensorium wore through, in exactly a year he would wake into another recycling day, once again faceless, and do it all over again.

THE GESTURE OF
TURNING A MASK AROUND

From his desk, and through his mask, Paolo watched the Grand Canal dissolve almost imperceptibly into the same oily darkness as the night. This process occurred only after the shimmering ribbon of water held on to the twilight's rich blues for as long as possible. When distracted, as he was tonight, Paolo would try to identify the precise moment that the water decided to finally relinquish the very last shadowy hint of blue, and surrender, once again, to black. But this only seemed to happen when he blinked, since he could never quite observe the final transition. It was then, when the bleeding of day into night was complete, that Paolo finally pushed his chair back, engaged his stiffened knees, and started methodically lighting the candles attached to a large chandelier leaning against the wall, perched at an angle, like an abandoned, ornate wagon wheel. This chandelier had once been the centerpiece of the magnificent ballroom of the palazzo in which he now lived and worked, alone. But since the Exodus, two of the three floors had been flooded with the warm, salty waters of the Laguna Veneta. And all that remained habitable of the palazzo — at least for humans — was now a single story, perched above the ever-rising tides. Indeed, sometimes, during especially high tides, or storms, the water would begin to seep through the floorboards of his room, as if beginning to sweat in the summer heat, or, alternately, bringing bad tidings of a winter fever. Paolo slept in a hammock, as had become the widely adopted custom of the city, which only enhanced the impression of living in a creaky ship. He would drift off to the lapping sound of the impatient sea, and sometimes even the enigmatic cries of seals, or the violent splashes of unfathomable sea creatures, new to these waters. Upon waking, he was sometimes surprised to find all the buildings moored where they had been the night before; half-expecting one of his neighboring dwellings to have sailed off over the horizon in the night.

After lighting a dozen or so candles — which groped outwards at odd angles, protruding from the paint-chipped skeleton like exotic fungi — Paolo put on a second coat over the one he was already wearing, and then returned to his desk, and the papers which awaited his wandering attention. The restless candlelight threw his dancing shadow on the wall, in marked contrast to his profound passivity. He wore a classic Bauta mask — the favorite of Casanova, it is said — which allows the wearer to talk, sip, or chew, without compromising one's identity. The flickering wall was covered in masks of all kinds, which appeared to watch him, like grotesque trophies of different possible selves. The Carnival officially began the day after tomorrow, but already some members of the public could be seen removing their masks, albeit surreptitiously; impatient for the festivities to begin. Indeed, just this wintry morning, Paolo had been walking home with a canvas bag full of stunted carrots and half-moldy cabbage, when a quick motion behind a window, one flight above him, caught his eye. He had stopped in his tracks, arrested by the image of a woman in an elegant Colombina mask, sipping from a glass of champagne, and playing the coquette for someone else in the room. A man wearing a long-nosed Zanni façade soon joined her by the window, and she offered her graceful neck to him. The man was obliged, however, to remove his disguise, in order to place his lips upon her pale skin. Paolo couldn't help but feel a surge of indignation at seeing the man's naked face; but could do nothing while they were behind closed doors. Nevertheless, he fixated on this romantic tableau until the protagonists of the impromptu scene noticed him watching. Paolo then proceeded to make an exaggerated warning gesture to the man, exhorting him to replace the mask. The man bowed ironically, but followed these mimed instructions, while the woman curtsied with an air somewhere between the obedient and the mocking. Paolo then continued on his way, perturbed.

Such scenes, when he stumbled upon them, affected him more than his fellow Venetians, for Paolo held the important and demanding position of Masquerade Master: a burden which, of course, reached a peak during Carnival. Since the Exodus, Venice had changed a great deal, to the extent that it was almost unrecognizable. Most of the city's inhabitants had fled inland, once the sea permanently covered the piazzas and pathways, leaving only the most stubborn and desperate souls to deal with the damp and unheated quarters in the winter, and the clouds of mosquitos in the summer. For every soul remaining, there were at least ten bedrooms to choose from, albeit ones increasingly at the mercy of the elements. Indeed, many of those who lived in the city were new arrivals, tempted by the lack of laws and landlords: often refugees from North Africa, the Middle East, and Far Eastern Europe. Resourceful carpenters and ingenious amateur construction workers had built a network of fixed planks and gangways between buildings, to allow — on a good day — dry-footed passage through the city. Younger locals often relied on spider-webbed rope ladders or bristling thickets of winches to scale from place to place, their hands permanently calloused or blistered; while some older folk relied on these very same young people to keep them alive, since the less nimble were now effectively trapped in their homes. Electricity was scarce, skimmed from the solar froth or scooped from pirate water-mills when possible, and subsequently rationed out as part of an elaborate, and often unsavory, barter economy (which co-existed with the circulation of crumpled Euros, or tattered American dollars).

But some things had not changed. Gondolas still cut swan-like trajectories through the soupy canals. The gondoliers themselves, sweating beneath their masks, even in the colder months, no longer fished for tourists — most of whom had fled with the last formal forms of sanitation — but for the hardy citizens of the new, ad-hoc Republic. On moonless nights the gondolas would become the main source of light for anyone brave enough to walk through the makeshift rigging of the city, thanks to the hissing gas-lamps or guttering lumps of tallow affixed to their prow. The Carnival also provided some measure of continuity for the city, along with the mask-making tradition that had once made it so famous. Indeed, Paolo's job was to coordinate the policing of mask-wearing in public; a vexed affair, with a long history. Throughout the centuries, different authorities had attempted to control the fixed visages of the festival, often prohibiting all forms of incognition, beyond the fortnight preceding Ash Wednesday. In more lenient epochs, Venetians were free to conduct themselves in disguise for much of the year. Today, however, two decades after the Exodus, the mask-making guild (still known as the mascherari), were one of the most influential groups in the city. The recently deposed Doge, who ruled the New Venetian Republic with a loose but erratic hand from the converted domes of St. Mark's Cathedral, insisted that masks only be worn during Carnival, in an attempt to make the inevitable gambling dens more transparent, in terms of who was fleecing who, and to avoid further street crime. The power of the mascherari, however, bolstered by newly-brokered links to the Mafia, had swiftly ensured that this tyrant be replaced by one of their own, who zealously implemented a decree that not only allowed the wearing of masks at all times in public, but imposed it. True, citizens were free to remove their masks in their own homes, provided their faces were not visible in the window. As a result, many locals embraced the habit of applying elaborate make-up under their masks, to discourage an unpleasant visit from Paolo's enforcers, come evening.

Paolo himself, as we have seen, would even conduct his affairs at night and indoors, behind one of the city's famous prosthetic faces, stylized and impersonal. Often he even slept in one of his two dozen masks, as a gesture of commitment to his role and responsibilities. Paolo was not a man to risk breaking rules that he had been tasked with upholding. And yet, he was secretly sympathetic to the residents of Venice, who lamented that Carnival had lost its special allure when essentially extended throughout the entire year. If the masquerade is permanent, then there can be no sense of relief, release, or suspension. The mask-making guild was certainly living more comfortably than most of those huddled in this rotting urban shipwreck; many of whom eyed the countless rats with a gnawing hunger. What surprised the new Venetians most, perhaps, was how quickly it felt troubling — or even obscene — to be confronted with the face of a fellow human, uncovered by plaster and paints. And yet this surprise too submerged into the general commerce of things, as the current arrangement began to feel as natural as the wearing of trousers, shirts, cloaks, or shoes. After all, why should the face be naked to the world? Were we not the only species smart enough to figure out the social and evolutionary advantages of fig leaves, armor, disguise?…And besides, many of the newer masks were designed to house a specially-scented wadding beneath the nostrils, which would provide some olfactory relief from the overpowering pungency of the sodden streets and squelching squares.

Reflecting thus on his charge, Paolo returned to the paperwork that had prompted his mind to be so restless in the first place. The first leaf of paper announced a report from one of his more reliable scouts, who had recently overheard a conversation in a popular tavern. This conversation suggested subversive elements were agitating for revelers to forsake masks during the Carnival: a protest, the author of the report opined, with the potential to turn the entire system around. On its own, this intelligence would have aggravated Paolo, but not overly concerned him, since such rumors had been circulating for a couple of years now. Several other papers on his desk, however — from different emissaries, in different quadrants of the city — had been reporting the same thing. It seemed as if the idea was gathering momentum. And it was his responsibility to stop this idea, before it became as powerful as a surge tide.

Feeling the weight of this challenge, Paolo rubbed his chin under the mask, which made a soft scratching sound, due to his evening stubble. For a moment his attention was captured by one of the many canal fires beyond his window, probably started by a gondolier's candle or gas lamp, coming into contact with a floating oil slick. But a soft knock at the door broke his flickering reverie. Glancing at his pocket watch, he was gratified to see that his housemaid and cook was delivering dinner precisely when instructed. The young woman, who timidly entered with a tray of food, was wearing a very simple mask, known as a *servetta muta*: a discreet black oval made of velvet. She held this disguise into place by biting down on a small ivory button, sewn into the back of the mask, which her mouth now considered as native to its intimate environs as her tongue or teeth. Given this arrangement, Paolo had yet to hear his maidservant's voice. (Though on slow days he daydreamed of what it *might* sound like, especially in the throes of an overwhelming pleasure, that he himself was providing her. But his many duties, and pious instincts, kept him from ever acting on this fleeting caprice.) The Masquerade Master gestured to the table near his hammock in a habitual and superfluous way, since the maid had placed his tray on this same surface for months now. Paolo's nostrils registered the scent of the boiled carrots and cabbage that he had foraged that morning, as a cover for his assignations with local informants. He hoped that his mute employee had been diligent in removing the moldy cabbage leaves before throwing the others in the soup.

Unusually, he took a moment to observe his maid, who was standing near the door obediently, head bowed, and waiting for further instructions or permission to withdraw. Once again, he noticed her shapely silhouette, and felt a sudden primal thrill, interlaced with more subtle feelings regarding the ever-contingent asymmetries of station.

"Child," he said, using the generic term he had taken to addressing her by. The maid seemed to sense the sudden tension of the moment in his tone, and lifted her gaze.

"Child," Paolo said again, enjoying her suspense. "We are indoors. There is no law forbidding me drawing the curtains, and instructing you to remove your mask."

Here the double-cloaked official heard an audible intake of breath, perhaps through delicate nostrils. He had a sudden, overpowering urge to see his domestic's naked face, after never giving her identity a second thought.

"You see," he continued, "I would like to ask you something. But this is impossible with your *muta* in place." This was indeed the first time Paolo had considered posing his maid a question; since habitually the flow of information and instruction was in a single direction, from his lips to her ears.

Paolo sensed that the young woman suspected that this was some kind of trap, and became impatient with her hesitation. Stepping forward, he could feel the warmth of her body in the chilly room, and slowly lifted his hands to remove the object between his gaze and the young woman's upturned face. While the features thus revealed stopped short of coalescing into that enigmatic form of defiance known as *beauty,* the paleness of her winter skin, the creaturely twitch of her nose, and the slight trembling of her lips, struck Paolo with a transgressive force; as if he had disrobed this maiden completely, against her will. Her hazel eyes — the only part he was familiar with — seemed smaller, unframed by the mask, yet more penetrating, for they looked at him directly, hoping for cues to help her navigate this unfamiliar interpersonal terrain.

For an extended moment, Paolo found himself resisting the urge to take off his own mask, and kiss this simple, denuded, fresh-faced girl. But instead he returned the mask to the woman's hand, stepped back towards his desk, and asked the question which had been troubling him.

"Tell me, child. Do you hear whispers in the streets about people taking off their masks for Carnival?"

The maid stood silent for a long while, as if her lips had been permanently clasped by the button which Paolo had just removed from her lips. He silently remarked upon the composition of the moment: the young woman's public visage now neutralized, held fast by her left hand, next to her hip, like any inanimate object.

"Well child?" Paolo snapped, when it was clear the cat had her tongue. "Speak up! Either you have or you haven't."

"No," came the quiet reply, after another pause; its single syllable already suggesting some kind of accent, a hundred miles or so to the East.

Talking like this — mask-to-face; he had almost forgotten how confronting it was, to attempt a conversation with the distraction of the interlocutor's identity, hanging there in the room, like an unspoken provocation, demand, or even insult. Social interaction proceeded so much more smoothly when the agents involved presented accepted and familiar archetypes. To stand like this, in front of the quivering and unnervingly mobile flesh of an actual face…well, it was most disconcerting. Paolo preferred his interactions to be impersonal, and not complicated by individual expressions. And yet, his physical being, at least, could not deny the charge that unmasking this woman had sparked in him.

"No rumors at all about this?" he probed further. "Not even in the laundry quarter?"

"No," she repeated, in a tone precisely mid-way, he thought, between truth and falsity.

"Very well," Paolo said, at last. "You may replace your mask and go."

The young woman's tongue quickly darted out between her lips, instinctively preparing them once again for the ivory button. She then eclipsed her visage with the dark *papier-mâché* moon that so often followed her orbit precisely, and exited the room like a shadow composed of discreet relief.

Paolo felt the young woman's human absence, and slumped back into his desk. He had no appetite, so let the soup squander its warmth. Reaching behind his weary head, he untied the black ribbon that kept his own mask in place, and then removed it; placing the delicate object gently on top of the papers in front of him. Meditating mindlessly for a while on this object, his attention was suddenly seized by the reverse side of the mask.

How unfinished it seemed! And how disorienting this vision became. The more he focused on the rough texture and warped contours, the more it seemed as if he were contemplating something prohibited; something which should not be exposed to too much light or attention. To sever this unnerving sensation, he pulled out a shaving mirror from his desk drawer, and looked into the reflection of his own naked face; asking himself the age-old question: is this not also a mask? And what of its *verso,* to his mortal *recto*? Only when he himself is no longer, Paolo realized with grim conviction, and fully decomposed, will another be able to see through his eyesockets, should they choose to make a *memento mori* mask from his remains.

Eventually breaking the gaze of his morbid narcissism, the weary official looked up at his wall of masks. They seemed to be jeering his lonely epiphany; daring him to turn them all around, and thus countering the forces of deception and deflection sealed into their structure. The *mascherari* were sorcerers, he concluded, not without admiration; forging one form of power in the mask itself, and another in the edict for the Venetian populace to wield such power without prudence — to effectively replace their faces, for all intents and purposes. The city was a vast puppet show. And he, Paolo, had his hand on one of the most significant strings. (Just as *his* wrists and ankles would suddenly twitch into life at the behest of the Doge, sitting in his throne, one mile to the North.)

With the foretaste of citywide subversion on his tongue, Paolo moved to the window, bare-faced, where any passing stranger could see him. He was almost disappointed to see the suspended streets outside empty, save for a boy of about ten years, and a mangy mutt, hopping around the little lad's heels. The boy was wearing a plague doctor mask, too big for his head, so that it almost seemed to devour him. Paolo watched, intrigued, as the boy performed a strange and stylized dance, as if on an Oriental stage, many centuries ago. The dog was trying to join in, with his own clumsy limbs. The boy began to laugh at his furry companion's antics. He then took his own mask off, and used the elastic to affix the grim shell over the dog's slobbering face. The boy began to waltz with the dog, now transformed into a grotesque and uncanny creature: half animal, half ghoul. But the dog had no patience for this encumbrance to his breathing and barking, and scratched it off his muzzle so violently that it crashed off the gangway and into the canal.

Both boy and dog watched the mask bob in the black water for a moment, before it swirled and sank under the slick surface. And then, as if of one mind, they swiftly disappeared themselves into the damp darkness of the city.

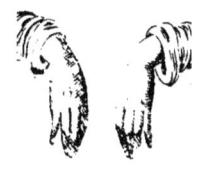

The Gesture of Planting

A man visited a small museum in a small city in the hour just before closing, and he made his way to a small room full of statuary and hid inside a stone vase until the room fell quiet and the lights went out and he was certain that he was alone.

He climbed out of the vase and brushed himself off and unzipped the knapsack that he had sneaked into the room, and took out a large, heavy hammer.

The man moved methodically from stone bust to stone bust, first stretching or kneeling to whisper into its ear, and then looking into its eyes to make sure that it had heard him. He then lifted the hammer and brought it down over and over again until he had smashed the bust to powder. He was a strong man, but it took him all night to do this. By the morning the man was surrounded by small piles of stone, each holding a dusty secret, and he used the hammer to bar the door of the only entrance to the room and put his head down on the floor and went to sleep.

After some days of banging on the door, the tired people who worked at the small museum in the small city realized that the man would not come out until he was ready, and they stopped banging and began instead to pass him thin packets of thin foods and thin skins of water under the door. He always accepted the water, and he always refused the food. Weeks passed this way.

The man took only a sip or two from each water skin, and he moved from pile to pile giving the rest to his stony garden. Each day, he watered the stone, and watched, and waited, until one day he saw the first shoots begin to sprout from the rock. And he watered, and watched, and waited, as his plantings matured around him.

The first stone stalk that rose from the ground ended with a bud in the shape of a clenched fist. As the stone fist opened, he recognized the hand of his mother, and he grasped it, and then he turned to the second pile of stone. (Into the ears of this one, he had whispered a childhood nightmare: a house, and a bed, and abandonment.)

The second pile had grown into a bed of stony moss, tiny stalks ending in bits of blanket or foot or eyelash that together made the shape of a sleeping woman. He stroked her hard hair with the tip of his thumb, and turned to the third pile. (This one had listened as he whispered his fear that he did not know how to love.)

The next had grown into a tree that ended in a sheared stump set with precious stones in the shape of a place setting: one plate, and one fork, and one knife, and one glass of wine. He bent to touch his lips to the crystal edge of the glass, and he moved on. (These ears had heard him confess his fear that he would grow old alone.)

And on, and on, he spent an evening moving from plant to stony plant, tending and touching the garden of his fears — of his history, of himself — made manifest. When he had finished, he moved through the room once again. He plucked the first stone stalk, and took the hand in his mouth, and chewed it, and swallowed, and placed the empty stalk on the floor. He gnawed the parts of the sleeping woman from their mossy bed, and sucked the plate, fork, knife, and glass from their stony table. And on, and on, he savored each course of his meal until falling, sated, in a pile of rocky leaves and roots and branches, and closing his eyes, and falling asleep.

After days without contact, the tired people who worked at the small museum in the small city finally managed to break down the door to the room. When the dust cleared, they found the stone busts arranged just as they'd left them, but one had sprouted the man's brown hair, and one stared out with his eyes, and one's lips had turned to the man's warm flesh. The man himself was nowhere to be found.

THE GESTURE OF PLANTING

"Where did I come from?" Anouk asked her mother.

This was hardly the first time that the young girl — following her mother about the house like a mischievous shadow, cast shorter than its source by a mid-day sun — had asked this question. And her mother, being the kind of person who believes in initiating the young into the true mysteries of life at an early age, repeated the same answer she had given the time before, and the time before that.

"Your father put his seed in me," she said matter-of-factly, scanning the bookshelf for a cover that only she would recognize.

Anouk smiled the same smile she smiled the time before, and the time before that. Indeed, she liked hearing this, because of the image it gave her. She pictured her father placing a seed, the size of a peanut, rather seriously and ceremoniously, under her mother's tongue. In Anouk's mind's eye, her father would then gently close her mother's mouth, like a purse, before giving her a soft kiss on the forehead for good measure, to symbolically complete the transaction. Anouk then imagined her mother cooking, driving, walking along the beach — even sleeping — all the while with this seed under her tongue; a tiny kernel preventing maternal speech for a whole month, by which time the little object was finally swallowed, now softened enough to blossom. Anouk pictured a tiny shoot then starting to push its way out of her mother's belly button, like the tentative uncoiling of a fern, quickly growing, day-by-day, into a little bonsai tree, eight inches high: a development obliging her mother to lie down for the last few months, and watch the tree grow nearly to the ceiling. Among the leaves fluttering in the air-conditioned breeze, Anouk would picture a fuzzy coconut, in which she — Anouk — was lying encurled. And no matter how many times her mother tried to detail the true biological processes involved, Anouk could not help but stray back to the vision of the peanut and the fern and the bonsai tree and the coconut.

Indeed, this stubbornly persistent image of her own genesis informed Anouk's entire cosmological outlook; especially regarding the other beings that crossed her path, whether they be sentient or not. Even before she began her formal schooling, Anouk had a profound hunch that every worldly thing existed by virtue of the gesture of planting. And by logical extension, she could create more of such things by finding the right seed. Thus, in order to procure the family cat a new playmate, she planted some of her own grey fuzzy socks in the garden, and diligently watered them with a red plastic watering can. When a stray cat appeared on their porch a month later, frazzled and hungry, Anouk smiled to herself, confident that this wary apparition was on account of her own green-thumb.

After that successful experiment, the garden soon looked as if it had been overtaken by an army of moles, as the formerly green grass gave way to clumps of dirt, under which were buried an entire cabinet's worth of curiosities. Having quizzed her parents, uncles and aunts, and two different babysitters about the secret lore of planting, she began to get a sense of the essentials of the ecological alchemy which *brings things into being*. From what the grown-ups told her, she gleaned that cereals, vegetables, fruits, and nuts were the most common things to be planted. Apparently there was a special breed of person dedicated to this task, called a farmer: a vocation which she instinctively had enormous sympathy for; although she was unclear as to why they would narrow their crops to *these* specific items, when there were so many other options to cultivate.

And so she sowed.

Having picked up bits and pieces — scraps of knowledge swept off the kitchen table-top like crumbs — Anouk discovered that one could also plant bulbs. And so a new mound of dirt appeared in the garden, underneath which lay a 60-watt lightbulb, from which she hoped would sprout a lamp-post; or even an entire powerplant, if left to grow at its own pace for long enough. Under another pile of dirt lay interned a humble sparkplug, from which she hoped to soon harvest a Honda Accord. (Or perhaps a Harley Davidson, depending on this metallic seed's provenance.) After being told of subterranean tubers, Anouk stole a toy trumpet and several kazoos from her kindergarten shelves, and buried them with some mulch, in the hope of harvesting an entire crop of brass instruments, glowing golden in the dawn like corn; an occasional F sharp or B flat scaring the bees, when the wind gusted in a certain direction.

Anouk planted a dozen eggs in a row, hoping to sprout some long-legged birds — regal stalks of storks — waving lazily in the breeze. And one evening, to the utter dismay of her baby-sitter, she buried an entire jar's worth of fire-flies, muttering something or other about "lightning seeds."

Of course, when nothing actually grew, Anouk was forced to play host to disappointment, and was then obliged to face the limits of her childish assumptions. She was forced to see herself, moreover, as the product of gestation, rather than plantation. Even so, whenever she happened to notice a dog burying a bone, she half-expected an elaborate skeleton to start sprouting from the soil, ready for display at the Natural History Museum.

Over time, Anouk learned to accept that the gesture of planting was just one among many explanations for how the bewildering variety of forms on this earth came to be. Beyond reproduction she learned about replication, construction, fabrication, engineering, and many other modes of manufacture. She learned about the traditional distinction between *nomos* and *phusis,* culture and nature, the organic and the artificial. And yet, Anouk was never completely comfortable with such distinctions; feeling deep in her marrow that all these varied ways of ushering new things into the world could be folded back into the humble, miraculous compression of the seed. The vase of a Venetian glassblower existed by virtue of the lungs, certainly. But there was at least a mental seed in the artisan's mind, inspiring him to ever more exquisite exhalations.

At university, Anouk experimented with hydroponics, until her little rented studio was filled to the brim with bright green vegetation. Leaves tickled her nose when she slept, and thick rubbery stems curled around her like amorous fingers. After taking art classes alongside earth sciences, she bought a vintage camera, experimented with various exposures, and then buried the negatives in terracotta pots outside her window. These she watered out of habit, half-expecting a miraculous form of photosynthesis to occur — a bouquet of captured images to sprout and develop under the sun's rays, breathing themselves into quivering, verdant, oxygenated life.

Unsurprisingly, Anouk selected for herself a vocation with an intimate connection to the soil: viniculture. She invested in a modest plot of land in Languedoc, along with the strong and simple man who sold it to her. She then spent several months sampling different kinds of grapes growing in the region, and especially chewing on their bitter seeds, confident that this would give her a truer sense of each one's essence and potential than any given single vintage which relied on its juices. In the end, she settled on some rare old vines from several valleys to the West. The gesture of planting in Spring gave way to the gesture of harvesting in Summer which in turn faded into the gesture of clearing in Autumn. The scent of the dried vines burning at dusk gave Anouk a numinous feeling; a mood suspended like the mellow smoke of this pagan incense.

After a sudden illness, Anouk's father passed away, and she suspended work to attend the funeral, and help her mother move in to the three-room "chateaux," perched above the vineyard. As others wept at the sight of the coffin descending into the ground, Anouk had watched dry-eyed, but heart-bursting, for she understood that her beloved papa was preparing himself to be reborn as a tree. A tree which sighs and hums and whispers, protecting passing creatures from the rain.

Unable to sleep, and in honor of his metamorphic journey, Anouk crept by candlelight to the cellar, where the liquefied fruit of her labor snored silently in rows. Four score and eight bottles — one, by sheer chance, for each year her father had lived as a person on this earth. Walking slowly around the cellar, cool and damp, as if Time Itself had condensed there, banishing the fetid centuries separating the various vintners who had toiled in this place, Anouk caressed the bottles gently; watching over them like a sentimental nurse in a hospital ward. For this is how she saw her cellar at night; the plum-colored bottles lying in rows like wounded soldiers, freshly returned from the front, bursting with sacrificial blood. Anouk, like all of her compatriots, knew that the soil was nourished by the brave, foolish, terrified bodies of her ancestors. She knew that to drink wine is to drink the blood of the namelessly crucified, and somehow redeem them. Wine is, after all, a totem drink in her country: a form of deep bodily remembering, and unconscious resurrection.

To plant and cultivate wine is, therefore, the ultimate act of optimism, infused with a resigned nihilism specific to her race. "We shall live to drink another day," this act says. "Though we will be drinking the mineralized bones of our own bloodless futures."

The taste of wine is the intoxicating taste of death, delayed one more day, at least.

And the tang of *terroir* is a pleasure fermented in a now-muffled terror, soaked deep into the soil.

Such were the dark, yet strangely fortifying, thoughts of Anouk, as she communed amidst her bottles, before creeping back upstairs and into the house, to curl up next to her wheezing mother.

"Maman," she whispered, without waking the old woman. "Where did I come from?"

And tucking a lock of grey hair behind her mother's ear, she answered her own question with a ventriloquil whisper.

"Your father put his seed in me."

THE GESTURE OF SHAVING

She sat in the grass and readied her space: a blanket, a bowl of water, a towel. A cheap pink disposable razor. She wore nothing but her hair. (Parts of her head and body were covered with a soft down, other parts bristled in little thickets of coarse brown.)

She dipped razor in water and brought it to her right ankle, slowly pulling the blade across her skin and taking a sudden involuntary breath as shivers of pleasure moved up her leg. She repeated the motion with her left ankle, and shuddered as the wave of skin joining foot to leg was opened cold to the air. She swished the razor in the bowl.

Some called her a wind artist. They asked her about this — What did it mean to be a wind artist? Why make works of art that no one could see, that no one but her could feel? The wind is my lover, she would offer in response. When you read a love poem do you not feel it wash over you? Watch me at my work, tell me what you feel. And they did watch. And each time she went to the grass she found one more person, or maybe two, sitting a respectful distance away, having brought their own blankets, and bowls, and towels, and razors, watching her and trying to make a copy of her work for themselves. But loving the wind is much too easy and much too difficult, and her work was not reproducible.

She pulled the razor to her throat and drew it gently down in long arcs. As each spot was freshly shorn, the wind rushed in with a kiss until it had whispered a necklace around her neck and blown breezy earrings for her ears. She closed her eyes and sighed and swished the razor in the water, and brought it to her left wrist, and pulled it across the top of her skin from hand to elbow, and when she had finished she did the same with her right arm. And so the wind draped her in tall, chilly gloves, and when she closed her eyes she felt them covered in tiny feathery clouds he had swept up for her in the course of his travels.

She had been a gardener once, an artist of green and growth. She would return home from a day in her studio, stained and exhausted from the slow waiting. When she left the garden, she pledged to herself that the next one she loved would be quicker, rougher, more volatile.

She brought the razor to her eyebrows, and she pulled it down and down and across until her face was a portrait in windy kisses.

And it went that way until she was all bare touched skin.

And then she stuck out her tongue and glided the razor across it. When she opened her mouth he slid inside her breath, and she held him there for as long as he would stay, and when she exhaled he left a coolness that dissipated through her as she watched him leave to run his fingers through the wild mane of a tree, wresting loose leaves from its branches and moving on as they floated down onto her bare scalp as mementos of his visit.

She was careful not to ask too much of her visitor.

She had known a glass artist, a water artist, an artist of stone. (One had cold skin covered in cuts. One had cold skin covered in bruises. One had drowned.) Their tools were not her tools, their preparations not hers. To love glass was blood and ice. To love stone was silence and pain. She had once watched the water artist at work: so similar to her own methods but with a stillness and a submerging that she could not manage. It was not for her.

One day she would move on from this work. On that day, she would share a morning with her lover — her material, her windy clay — before taking out a fresh blade and nicking her arms and legs and belly and watching the red rivulets course over the skin she had prepared for him, knowing at that point he would turn away from her and she would move on to work in rain, or fire, or fur. But today she packed up her things, and stood in her smooth nakedness, and blew him a kiss that would find and become part of his body, and walked home.

THE GESTURE OF
SHAVING

The hairy man moved slowly around the kitchen, looking for the jar of instant coffee that usually sat obediently on the bench near the gas stove. He had the same build as my father, and even the same eyes and nose, but he lacked most of the face. Cheeks, chin, and much of the neck was covered in coarse black hair. Watching from the kitchen table, as I scooped up errant pieces of puffed rice floating in milk, I watched this creature — both strange and familiar — with a wary eye. The hairy man had returned from a long trip like this, carrying my father's suitcases. He even had the nerve to kiss my mother when he entered the house. I noticed with glum surprise that she did not seem to object. Indeed, the hairy man scuffed my own hair playfully — the blond mop on top of my head — just as my father sometimes did; and spoke to me in the same voice. But I merely shrugged and shifted away, squinting at this rather uncanny presence; my eyebrows the shape of a question mark, as I tried to catch my mother's ever-distracted gaze.

This was during the high era of hairy men: a time of many hirsute pursuits. Men's shirt collars bristled with a layer of human fur, crawling out the top, as if trying to colonize the neck. Beards and chest hair often grew towards each other, creating an entire carpet on the top half of a man's body. Follicles on every surface and in every crevice seemed to burst forth like black, brown, or grey grass; heavily seeded, and boosted by the human mulch below the skin. Male shoulders sprouted wings of keratin, thick enough (in many cases) to comb. Forearms were ensleeved in dark wool, and knuckles sprouted wispy sprigs. Tufts emerged from ears. Soft hairy stalactites grew down from flaring nostrils. From what I could gather as a very young boy — still hairless and voraciously curious about the grownups who presumed to be stewards of my fate — entire forests of hair would grow beneath men's clothing; filling the spaces under arms, above knees, and even (schoolyard rumor had it) between buttocks. Hairy men were everywhere. In restaurants. Walking in the city square. Grinning from billboards and sinning on TV. Thanks to snatches of conversation and a particularly confusing sexual education class — led by our school librarian, who did not cease blushing for a full hour — I understood that some Big Change lay ahead of me; a bit like becoming a werewolf, but the transformation would be permanent. That evening I stood in front of the bathroom mirror, and tried to picture my body, covered in coarse, animalistic coils. I tried to imagine my face — currently as smooth as a cherub's buttock — with first the manicured facial hair of the devil, and then the more comforting snow-white beard that I understood God to have — as if the Lord had first emerged from the clouds, and retained some of their cumulus.

Hairy men ruled the world, through the sheer multiplicity of their collective presence. If a specific hairy man was unavailable, another would surely do just as well. Indeed, who knows how they knew what to do, or who they themselves were, when they looked into the mirror and just saw a profusion of protein threads, covering their lives like fibrous creepers? Who knows how their wives or girlfriends recognized them at the end of the work day? These men seemed to be as indistinguishable as coconuts or shrubs. Human thickets, loosely connected by nicotine-stained fingers and an aimless conspiracy of the indistinct. Women and children, not nearly so entangled with the environment, tolerated the hairy men, for the most part; but trembled when the furry head-spheres opened to reveal an angry pink orifice, like errant flesh found inside a cyst. Profusions of hair matted and caked like neglected doormats. Confusions of wiry threads strung themselves throughout the land like tripwire or dangling cheese slicers, obliging us to step carefully and watch our heads.

Then suddenly, seemingly overnight, the culture changed, and the hairy men began to disappear at a rapid rate; as if an army of invisible lawn mowers had swept through the land, leaving a new occupying army of men-folk: smooth, shiny, and manicured. The newcomers displayed waxy chests and smooth shoulders. Different scents filled the air; less reminiscent of musk, cheese, spices, sebum, and whiskey, and more evocative of spray-canned florals and celery juice. A sudden mushrooming of pastel-neon jazz bistros played host to these new confident strangers, who had so quickly and efficiently chased away the hairy men.

Being a man of fashion, the hairy-man-who-was-perhaps-my-father succumbed to these new atmospheric pressures, and summoned me to the bathroom. Also being a person who liked to minimize missions, he decided to combine his own transformation with a life-lesson, explaining to me — as he filled the sink with warm water — that shaving was a rite of passage for any boy, and signaled the moment of becoming a man. As he lathered up the shaving brush against a large bar of soap, I instinctively felt my own cheeks with my hands, still smoother than a peach; closer perhaps to a nectarine. But I was to watch and absorb this most masculine process: the metamorphosis from bearded to clean-shaven. The lather was swirled around his cheeks, chin and neck, until the hairy-sudsy man looked like a grotesque Santa Claus, making strange expressions to himself in the mirror, as he twisted his lips and jaw this way and that, to give the razor more purchase on his sandpapered skin. As his elbow cocked at strange angles, he even seemed to be blowing kisses to himself in the mirror. At first, I had the strong sense that with each pass of the blade, the man's face was disappearing altogether; as if he was being diminished with each stroke. But my eyes slowly adjusted to the process, so that I saw, through the steam in the chilly bathroom, pale skin where tufts of hair bristled only a moment before. Stroke by stroke, and inch by inch, my father returned to the house, as I began to recognize the smooth geometry of his face, now only splattered with bits of white foam, and a tiny speck of blood near his left ear. By the time he rinsed his face, and toweled away any residues of the process, I was utterly convinced this presence was indeed my father, though I did not know how to express my relief, other than to blink more than before. He tussled my hair again, and handed me the shaving brush. "Here. This is yours now, for when you're ready. It's made of horsetail."

As my father hummed to himself in the bedroom, dressing for the day, I tried to follow his motions from memory, lathering up the brush once more, and covering my cheeks, chin, and neck with thick and creamy foam. I then meticulously moved the razor over my face until the suds were gone, nicking my skin only once or twice. Feeling like I had already passed some kind of milestone, I washed the invisible future-stubble down the drain; splashing myself with after-shave to smell like a grown-up. The sensation was of metaphysical precision, as if I had sharpened the line between me and the world. I was a shaved being, saved from anonymity.

That night I dreamed I lay on a stone table, in the middle of a forest. I stared up at the leafy canopy in a malaise, unwilling, or perhaps unable, to stand up. I could feel a thick beard growing faster than the ropes of ivy all around. I felt myself begin to merge with the forest, as the hair from my arms, legs, and face began to surge, extend, and twist around the ferns and tree roots. I was being absorbed by the world, or I was absorbing the world, I could not tell which, as the borders of my body began to blur and unravel. I was a burlap sack full of soil and seeds, sprouting at a demonic speed, meshing with the weeds. The sensation was not entirely unpleasant, and yet — deep within my slumbering psyche — a sense of panic began to grow. Even as part of me knew this was a dream, I feared I would not be able to wake up; and may never inhabit my contoured self again. I tried to pull the long beard from my face, with leaden arms, covered in fibrous tendrils, but this only made it longer, like a freakish carnival trick. And so I called out into the echoing forest for help. I could sense my heroic, clean-shaven father trying to find this part of the forest, machete in hand. Occasionally I could hear him call my name in the distance, but he could not hear or find me.

When I awoke, heart beating like a giant trapped moth, I was relieved to find my body had not really meshed with the sweaty sheets. I shaved three times that morning, and twice that afternoon, despite being at least four years away from puberty.

THE GESTURE OF
LISTENING TO MUSIC

Here is a room. There is a couch, and a rug, and a thin black music box, and a plain glass vase holding a red flower.

The woman walks to the couch and sits. She stares at the grey wool of the cushion, and as she looks her eyes turn grey, and the cushion looks back at her. She brushes her skin against the rough wool, and her fingers sink through it as she becomes part of the cushion and the fabric touches her bones, her meat, her small muscles.

The man walks to the woman on the couch. She hears him breathing and moves her attention to him, and wool unclasps skin and eyes turn brown as they unclutch the grey and as she feels his gaze on her body she feels eyes growing in her shoulders, her belly. She pulls her fingers from the couch and reaches for his mouth and watches her palm dissolve into breath and holds it out for him to bring into his lungs as tiny alveoli grow on her wrist. When he takes her finger into his mouth, her skin sprouts tastebuds and his tongue swirls into fingerprints and strokes her knuckle as her knuckle tastes his lips.

And when they kiss it is like this, lips and tongue and teeth dissolving into one another, and when they embrace it is like this, skin dissolving into skin dissolving into waves that break with and over each other.

She stretches her hand out of the small of his back and reaches for the top of the thin black box, and opens it. They listen as the pulse of the music begins to flow toward the couch, the grey wool turning darker, the cushions starting to ripple. As the waves of sound reach his knee, the skin flickers, and she touches it with flickering teeth and cheek. The sound turns their bodies to pulse and flow and flicker as she listens to the music of his thigh and he listens to the harmonies of her neck and her earlobe.

She turns her attention from him, just for a moment of coming-apart so that she can feel the tension of him before coming together again.

And when their voices rise from the mingling, they merge with the music so that the sounds of the thin black box come from their mouths, and they listen as the box sighs and purrs with pleasure. And when they call to the gods in gratitude for what they're feeling, the gods listen, and for a time the man and the woman are divine while the gods explode with desire and satisfaction.

Once they tire of being gods, the woman and the man close the music box, come unmingled, and find themselves in themselves once again. The woman pads across the rug and plucks the red flower from the vase and carries it with her to bed, where she lays it on the pillow and curls next to it and closes her eyes and brings her lips to its center and inhales deeply, and the man watches as soft red petals weave themselves into her eyebrows and lashes, and her breath begins to smell of roses, and her teeth turn to thorns, and as her hair plaits itself into green layered leaves he touches them and feels each of his fingers spreading into a thousand green strands. When he bends to whisper into the tiny pink bud of her ear, it blooms open for him, and when he hums the tune from the music box he feels her humming back, and as he listens his skin undoes itself and opens him to the tune as he dissolves into it with her. And they stay that way, joined in a becoming, until the man tires, and stops his whispers, and brings himself back into himself, and sinks to the floor and falls asleep.

Soon, he will wake into a cloud of red petals held aloft by the memory of her hums and his whispers. As he hears and smells and touches he will watch the parts of him slowly turn thin and soft and red as he becomes the cloud, just as the woman has before him. Years from now, a storm will rend their house from the ground and after it passes all that will be left in place of their home will be a garden of roses growing out of a mattress, each playing the same tune from the same old music box when the wind blows through their petals.

But not yet. Now, the man sleeps. And he dreams of a woman with skin made of music and grey woolen eyes.

The Gesture of Listening to Music

Dr. Challand.

You have asked me to keep a record of my thoughts, as a supplement to our discussions. Given how little diversion my life currently provides, I will indulge you — and myself — even though I cannot claim to be an engaging writer; nor even an attentive witness to my own mental states. No matter how banal or outlandish the content, I hope you see this exercise as a gesture of faith in your expertise, given that I would not agree to such an intimate form of communication with most of the other professionals to whom I have turned to in the past. And so I sit here in my study, the windows open on one of those early spring days in which hope promises (or should that be threatens?) to return, like a lover from one's banished youth; limping and faintly ridiculous, but welcome company nevertheless. I have a pot of tea brewing beside me, but just noticed that the cup I selected is chipped. Why mention such an insignificant detail? Because in doing so I might better ignore the fact that a starling is chirping in the birch tree in the garden.

The problem, as you know, has been distilled by you and your colleagues into a triple diagnosis. *Monomania. Melancholia. Melophobia.* (Three intimidating M's.) The first describes my

fixation. The second my inclination. And the third, my affliction. I am single-minded in my sorrow, and sorrowful in my
single-mindedness. We both know this. And yet it provides
some sense of perspective to write it down in black-and-white
(no doubt the reason you asked me to do so). I get to see myself through the professional gaze; along with the confident and
clearly shaped technical terms that attempt to seize and explain
the pitiful nature of my condition.

The most difficult lesson, perhaps, is the one in which we
learn that the universe is entangled, beyond all human capacity
to understand these clandestine connections. Meaning that if a
hapless soul, such as myself, tries to avoid one thing, she ends
up avoiding almost everything. For not only does one thing lead
to another, but each thing is inextricably bound to another, even
as the self attempts to detach from all of life's grasping tentacles.
(You see the irony here, as well as I, I'm sure.) In trying to avoid
music — a folly I've been earnestly attempting for over ten years
now — I must also elude all manner of things sympathetically
attached to music. For someone like myself, with skin made of
pure nerves, it is as if everything in life is connected by invisible
string, and if one object is tugged and toppled, in order to be
relieved of its presence, a swift chain reaction leaves everything
scattered on the ground. (I fear I'm already expressing myself
badly.) So to say, invisible spider webs — spun from the human
sense of impending dread — are woven around our ankles and
hearts, tripping us up when we step too far, or venture forth
with too much plan and purpose. Who knew that a profound,
visceral fear of music would lead, for instance, to an associated
fear of mirrors, for the simple reason that I cannot bear to see
what this original distress has done to my once fairly pleasant
face? Music — which I once adored above all the other intangible pleasures of life — has etched its bitter score into my skin,
and across my persecuted features. (I know this to be true! No
hollow compliments can distract me from the fact.) Indeed, no
sadist with a quill could have done a better job at carving lines in
my forehead than my own tortured thoughts. (But I *have* made

progress, Dr. Challand, since I write the word "music" now with only a shudder, rather than a dry panic!)

Yes. Progress. For here I am, scratching words upon a blank page, and my heart is merely skipping, rather than trying to escape the cage of my ribs. Something about this morning, and perhaps even this starling's song, is inspiring a fruitful kind of fatigue in me. (Another victory, Dr. Challand — as I just wrote the word "song" while sipping tea, without spilling a drop!) I no longer feel like twisting and turning away from myself, or the people I pay to put up with me. There is something soothing about the act of writing; in its silence, in its honest distance from music. Writing is frank, even when it tries to convince, persuade, or mislead. One can see it — one can take its measure, by the eye and with reason. (Poetry, of course, attempts to smuggle the spirit of music into the body of the text, to varying degrees of success, which is why I avoid the masters of cadence and prosody.) The clean and crisp letters of the alphabet provide strong structures for mutual comprehension; like the frame of a house, or the bones of our bodies. Music, on the other hand, is invisible. It refuses to be arrested, even when captured by a gramophone recording. The obscene orchid-shaped trumpet ejaculates sound, when the needle touches the disc, but we cannot catch this vibrational bile in a bucket, for further investigation; should we even want to. Music is the most duplicitous of aesthetic seductions, and it is no coincidence that the Sirens used song to lure men to their death. (I often have nightmares where I am, like Ulysses, strapped to the prow of a ship, and unable to stop the music entering my ears, my mind, my soul.)

Did all this begin with the father, as your science insists? Or the mother? I am sorry to disappoint you on this score, but my own trauma did not occur until I was a young woman. (Unless we consider the possibility that the seeds of this ordeal were planted as an infant, eventually leading me to be attracted to the kind of person who…. who…well…isn't this the crux of it? The talking cure — or in this moment, the attempted writing cure — always breaks down at the moment of most significance. It is impossible to confront the monster face to face, without being destroyed by it; or at least damaged further. But this is precisely what I intend to do, fortified as I am by Earl Grey, and an unseen bird that is mercifully avoiding devolving into melody.)

Perhaps I should stop here. Perhaps I have had enough "excitement" for one day. But no. I believe I am finally ready to tell a lurid tale: The Story of the Man Who Made Me This Way. The True and Authentic Account of He Who Ruined Me. (Or if not this, I at least feel ready to acknowledge that there is a definite tale to be told here.) The curtain rises to reveal a gay young woman; no better or worse than any other of this time and tribe. Thinking back, I am fond of this young woman, and wish to warn her of what she would become. For I had days of compassion, just as I had days of self-absorption. I occasionally sinned, even as I prevented others from sinning, when their eyes asked me to do so. When I met the man who carried my fate in his pockets, I thought I had already known love several times. In fact, I had only been brushed by its indifferent wing. In this case, however, I was to be devoured by its jagged beak. He was charming. A composer from one of those small, hilly European towns that produce more than their fair share of personified genius. We met at a concert hall where he was being celebrated for his second symphony, which was taking London by storm. I fell for his voice first, I believe, which was deep and resonant, like a cello, tense with resin. His eyes were restless: pleading and insolent all at once. Of course, I was powerless against a master of this, the most fundamental art of the muses. Over champagne and baked trout he explained to me his childhood epiphany: that he could in fact hear the music of the spheres, and channel it through human instruments. He explained to me that life is bathed in music, and even silence is a suspended form of harmony. During his sojourn in London, and as he openly courted me, his techniques became increasingly experimental. Soon enough, he was looking for music in places even the most bold and modern critics would find unmusical. He returned from a trip to Italy in an especially feverish mood, obsessed by a group of forward-thinking artists bonded through contempt for tradition, and who called the concert hall "a hospital for anemic sounds." Speaking of blood, I remember one occasion when I accidentally cut myself on the head of a nail, sticking out from a door frame. As soon as he noticed, he grabbed my hand with relish and sucked the blood off my finger. Closing his eyes, in an obscene sensual transport, he suddenly claimed to hear the melody that had hitherto been trapped in my veins. He then spent half the night transcribing it for harpsichord, viola, shrill soprano, and stockman's whip. (I fainted three bars into the piece, the first time I heard it "played" at a salon.)

However, when not deliberately assaulting the ears of innocent music lovers, he could make the most enchanting and exquisite compositions come to life on an intimate scale, as if drawing a mural for me in mid-air, with his own delicate and phosphorescent fingers. When in a tender mood, as would happen sometimes when we were alone, he would play the piano for me in a way that felt like he was caressing and massaging my tired limbs. When he played the violin, I felt as if it were my own hair stretched across the wooden bridge, producing shivers of pleasure down my neck. And when he played the flute, it was if he was breathing music over my entire being; as if my body had become an Aeolian harp, leaving my very soul with ticklish and prickling flesh. Had he been content to dwell in such moods, I would continue to welcome the moving power of music whenever I encountered it. Instead, I fled even the very possibility of its occurrence. If an organ grinder set up shop outside my window, I would have to impose on my weary sister's hospitality until I heard word that he had moved on. If a child began to whistle, I would glare at this simple urchin until their lips grimaced in confusion, thereby breaking the sound in two. So to say, when I finally managed to escape the spell of this man's suffocating presence, I soon realized that I would possibly be spending the rest of my days escaping any kind of sound which threatened to coalesce into an order or pattern. Trains were no longer a viable form of transport for me, given the rhythm of their movement. The chirping of birds drove me to distraction. And the morning song of shopgirls, on their way to work, would prompt me to take off my shoe as a missile (although I never let one fly).

For you see, when I regretfully refused his hand in marriage, for reasons too complicated to go into here, his compositions became increasingly obsessive, elaborate, and vengeful. While I attempted to remain a firm friend, perhaps even an illicit lover, he became sullen and sarcastic. I heard unpleasant rumors about underground concerts, in which startled young women would, only minutes into the performance, suddenly find themselves with bleeding noses, rushing from their seats in white dresses stained red. Even so, I agreed to be his "private ear," for new compositions, in the interest of salvaging our already tattered relationship.

This...this was the definitive period when he resorted to actual torture, through the instruments of his trade. (Who knew they could be so cruel?) Even in an auditorium, packed to the gills with polite society, he figured out a way to isolate me in the crowd, and beam the full power of his craft into a vindictive point, needling the ear and wheedling the mind. (I imagine this is where you take notes, Dr. Challand, concerning a delusional egoistic tendency. But I swear to you this is true. I don't claim to be special. But I *am* convinced that he had the power to pummel me into spiritual submission through his diabolical arrangements.) For you see, he spoke often of his impatience for any philosophy or system which separated the body from the soul. They were one and the same, in his eyes (and ears). And music was the proof. This approach to his musical works meant that he became a kind of unhinged surgeon, wielding a sonic scalpel with sadistic precision.

He took laudanum in increasing doses at this time, and spoke incoherently about Orpheus and Pythagoras, and the principle of *pathos*. I tried to make sense of his feverish lectures, as he would announce things grandly (or even worse, in a hissing whisper). Things like: "I will make the listeners' salivary glands vibrate in such a way as to think and feel the geometric structure of the fugue and so a logical aspect of the world as a whole." Or, at another time, "I will make the listeners' oral cavities oscillate in such a way they mentally experience unconditional, all-embracing love." To all appearances he succeeded in the latter, given that he swiftly gained an entourage of simpering girls and boys (as well as unsettling hybrids of both). Indeed, I have no doubt he succeeded in his devilish pact or pursuit, given that his concerts continued to persecute me in particular; making my teeth vibrate as if at the dentist, or my eyes water as if filled with smoke, or my stomach churn, as if pregnant with an incubus. During one particularly manic sonata, I confess with great shame, he even managed to bring me to an urgent physical climax, twenty rows away from the stage!…only to leave me cold, abandoned, and humiliated in the third movement. It was an act of pure spite. But there was no denying its force. Indeed, his power was such that I began to fear even the most innocuous melody, the most harmless and capricious ditty, in case it smuggled slivers of his malicious intent. I began to sense a bottomless well of dread lurking behind every attempt to beguile the ear; every instance of solicitous vibration. The gesture of music was as a consequence no longer a glorious thing. No longer a mode of reception, where the molecules of divine sound traced and affirmed the contours of the self in glowing, resonant affirmation. Instead it was a violation. An enforced opening. Exposure to a black ocean. Dissolution. My entire sense of self was like those metal plates covered in sawdust, across which a bow is drawn, making the particles dance into a cosmic shape latent in the vibrations themselves. Only in reverse. The clarity of my soul's silhouette was being drawn into blank anonymity.

And all this came to the point where…well…you know the rest, don't you, Dr. Challand. I'm sure I've already tested your patience with this rather breathless narrative. But I hope you see it for what it is: a good faith attempt at self-cure, with your calm support as inspiration. I dare say there is catharsis between these lines!

Indeed — yes, why not? — during my next appointment I urge you to enter the room humming! I do believe I could stand this, with only some modest gritting of teeth (provided the morning is as splendid as this one, with hope riding the sun beams like miniature foals). Not long ago, as you well know, I could not abide anyone taken with the act of humming. These people, humming a few bars of the latest popular song, as they measured out a half-pound of Turkish delights, or as they tapped their pencil on the *Times*'s crossword puzzle on the bus meant no harm, but they may as well have been agents of the devil to my former self. (You see what I just did there? I just placed some rational distance between my current self, and the woman who writhed with affliction. So I see: writing has its own kind of magic. It can chase away the shadows.)

Yes, Dr. Challand. I believe that I am improving. After all, just this morning I saw a photograph of a violin in a magazine, and did not even cover my ears.

THE GESTURE OF
SMOKING A PIPE

It was autumn and it was cold and she went out in the rain. She walked to a bench in the park and waited there until someone came. A man did come, and he was tall and smelled like cats. She sat with him for a while, silent and still with eyes closed while she tried to imagine herself into his pockets. Eventually she brushed the lint from her eyelashes and stood up and walked away until she came to a large dark puddle.

She bent down and sat beside it, and she waited for the rain to let up enough to still its surface, and when that happened she peered inside and looked for what looked back. When she recognized herself in the water — and this did not always happen, and certainly not right away — she closed her eyes and felt a splash on her face as a tiny frog hopped out of the puddle and sat on her knee and blinked up at her as she opened her eyes again.

She reached out to touch it. In that gesture of connection, once again she saw herself, and again she felt a splash as two more miniature green frogs hopped from the puddle and settled beside her. She sang to them — just a little — and as she heard herself in the song, she watched as the ground greened, covering itself with little hopping things birthing themselves out of splashes.

She looked around herself at the spreading carpet of small green gods with tiny frog eyes and small frog feet that she had called out of the earth in her acts of recognition. (Recognizing yourself is a rare thing, her mother had told her. It almost never happens. It happens all the time. It's the most normal thing in the world. It's a kind of magic. You have to be very patient, and very careful, and know how to look, and know where to watch. It can happen when you're not looking. It will turn you into a magician, her mother told her. You must try never to do it. You must do it as much as possible. You are a goddess, her mother told her. You are nothing special.) She scooped up handfuls of gods and stuffed them into her pockets until she couldn't fit any-more, and she nodded to the ones left behind and watched them disappear back into the puddle and got up and brushed leaves off the seat of her pants and wetly walked home.

Her tiny companions made the weather along her way. When a frog-god hiccuped, she heard a peal of thunder. Another one sneezed, and a tree fell over. As she walked past the man on the bench, he looked at one of the little gods and smiled, and when it smiled back the man felt heavy coins filling his hat and socks and mittens. When she walked past trees with the gods in her pockets, for a moment they each sparkled as if strung with lights, until she left them behind and the lights went out.

When she arrived at home, she scooped the gods onto the countertop and poured a plastic cup of bubble tea into a large saucer and watched as they hopped over to it and tried to bal-ance themselves on the tapioca pearls.

There were no mirrors in her house, no photographs or por-traits, no cameras, no laptops, no paper or pens, no magazines or books — nothing to record an image or a sound, nothing to convey herself to herself. She used to have all of these things and she nearly drowned in the clouds that would open up in the ceiling and pour down upon her every time she saw her own reflection in a glass or the description of a character in a story. Jellyfish gods rained down with the water, and her skin would sting with the bites of their long jelly arms. It was better when she was outside. Somehow the puddles helped. She found the frogs more manageable.

She sat down in the kitchen and fanned her fingers out on the table until she could just make out the faintest webbing starting to form between them. She bent her back until it was nearly horizontal, and as the little gods started jumping out of the saucer and over to her, she widened her eyes and they began to bulge out from her head. She opened her mouth, and one by one the gods jumped inside. When her cheeks were full with them and the saucer was empty, she closed her mouth and began to chew, tasting damp and pebbles and wood and leaves and smoke. As she swallowed divinity, her fingers unwebbed and her eyes receded back into her face and her skin lost its green tinge, and she got up and took herself to bed. That night she dreamed of the man on the bench. And when she woke up soaked, the bed and the floor obscured in a tangle of tentacles, she watched her eight fingers stretch and her knuckles grow suckers and she clicked the little beak forming on her lips, and she sighed, and she readied herself for breakfast.

THE GESTURE OF
SMOKING A PIPE

When I awoke, the children were pointing at me, their curious heads swiveling to their guardian for cues, and then back again. One of the urchins — a young boy of about nine — was holding a stick. Perhaps this was the source of the dream I had just been rudely wrested from, in which I had been pierced by several arrows, like Saint Sebastian, each one bringing its own form of bliss, deep within the burning. Had I been alone after such a nocturnal transport, I might have even checked my torso for evidence of night wounds. But now this clutch of children, which I counted quickly as twelve rudimentary souls, watched me with a collective wariness, as if waiting for me to provide something I had already promised them, but neglected to remember. I blinked the sleep out of my eyes, and turned my stiff neck to the guardian, a woman of approximately my own age — neither old nor young — who preferred to look out upon the lake, pricked by precipitation.

"Leave him be, children," she said, without conviction. "The man is clearly wanting for a home this gray morning, and is not likely to be warmed by your gawping."

I lifted myself to my elbows, as the children heeded their guardian's implicit advice, breaking off into little clusters, dividing their attention between myself and the scene beyond the open rotunda — a space usually reserved for summer concerts — in which I had spent the night. An insistent rain was falling, which was no doubt why this pensive group had taken shelter here, despite the vagrant snoring nearby. I noticed a martial line of silk parasols — most black, the remainder white — leaning against the railing in a puddle of their own making. The guardian offered a further comment, and the children recombined into a new set of somewhat reluctant groups. Two girls began to play a game involving the elaborate choreography and intertwining of hands, while another watched with envy. A fourth took out a small book from her shirt pocket, no bigger than a matchbox, and attached to the garment by a chain. A pencil produced from behind her ear was then used to record what only she could say, while stealing side glances at me, without excessive judgement. The boys fished in their satchels for marbles, and started to play earnestly, according to rules I was unfamiliar with.

Feeling increasingly aware of my own superfluous, yet heavy, presence, I pushed my thick coat, which had been serving as a blanket, aside, and attempted to unrust myself into society. The guardian grew weary of watching the lake exchanging different shadows of grey with the fog, and made a gesture of request to sit down, as if this sheltered space were my own. I opened my palm to encourage her to do so. She smiled without smiling, and then joined me on the stone bench, which followed the curve of the rotunda for half of its radius. She watched her charges for a while, occasionally offering admonishments or encouragements befitting their various activities.

"Can we catch the ferry today, Miss Lancaster?" asked one of the boys, tiring of marbles through a series of quick losses.

"I don't think so, Philip," said the guardian, "The day is against our outing, I fear. As soon as the rain lessens, we shall return to school."

The children did not audibly groan, preferring to let their heavy heads and slumping shoulders speak on behalf of muffled voices.

As if in response to the woman's plan, the rain began to fall with greater force, obliging the children to move closer under the humble pavilion, which in turn bound their blood-warmed energies in a more intimate cat's cradle of lines and hollows. One girl began to re-braid her friend's braids, while a new combination of glassy eyes began an impromptu card game.

The woman fished a scone from inside her coat and offered it to me. My stomach growled at the sight, and I thanked her sincerely for this blessing; the first breakfast I had enjoyed in three dawns. I noticed that her coat had more than the usual amount of pockets; no doubt for all the objects she might need to cater for the children on an outing such as this. I chewed on the scone with great satisfaction, as the children turned to whispering, as if the rotunda was a temple, opened on to the world. As I licked the crumbs off my fingers, the woman sighed at the state of the weather — or perhaps my ungentlemanly manners — and then produced a pipe from one of her many pockets. It was a large example of the form, made of dark Cherrywood, with an oriental curve. As before, she made a gesture of request, and I nodded my head in encouragement, as if to say "be my guest." With an expression of imminent contentment she tapped the bowl several times against the bottom of her left shoe, and then cleaned the stem with a piece of wire. A small tin full of fluffy and fragrant tobacco was then produced from yet another fold in her garment, along with a match, which — after bringing all the elements together in habitual harmony — she held to the bowl. The dried leaves glowed and crackled, as she inhaled and exhaled seemingly in unison, blowing out an aromatic smoke which left her lungs to join the nearby mist, adding a shade of blue to its dreary monopoly of the day.

"Are you just passing through?" she asked, exhaling smoke from her nostrils, and looking me in the eye for the first time.

"Well that depends," I replied. "I'm looking for work, and overheard some people saying that there are some jobs to be had here. That is, for a man who knows his way around a kitchen, as much as a factory."

Miss Lancaster nodded in vague sympathy.

"Well I wish you well on your search," she said, drawing deeply on the pipe. "I know how hard it is these days; especially now the South has lost its grid."

I leaned over to retrieve my pack, from which I produced my own pipe, made of smooth bone-colored ivory, which had been given to me by my grandfather: one of the few objects still in my possession of the many I once owned, and the one most charged with sentiment. The woman offered me her tobacco, to which I accepted also, feeling now twice in her debt. As I began to add my own smoke rings to the occasion, the children, one by one, began to produce small clay pipes from their pockets; all standard school issue, except for one or two exceptions, which had likely been gifted from an indulgent aunt or doting father.

All as one, and with a sense of profound calm, we puffed together, and felt the effects of the tobacco on our nervous systems, as the rain finally began to ease, and the obscured ferries groped their way across the water by way of occasional low, steam-powered whistles.

Then, at a single word from Miss Lancaster, the children tapped out the warm ashes onto the ground of the rotunda, cleaned and dismantled their pipes, before adding the necessary tension to their knees and elbows in order to reclaim their parasols, and trudge back along the lake front.

Feeling my own pipe, sleek and cooling in my hands, I watched these random sparks from the human furnace wind their way into the smudged landscape, until the mist raptured them away into a pillowy silence.

THE GESTURE OF
TELEPHONING

CLIMATE: FOUR TYPES OF WAITING

1.

We are watching a woman in bed.

There's a telephone on the bedside table, and she sits naked under the covers and she waits.

The phone rings.

She cannot hear it, but she can see the weather in the room changing: the lamp goes out with a pop of the lightbulb and the glass in the windows turns cloudy and the wood of the closet door dries and cracks and the carpet turns sodden and squeaky and she feels a wetness creeping up through the mattress and the skin of her hands whitens and crisps and the phone stops ringing.

She pushes the blankets away, and gets up, and unscrews the lightbulb and crushes it in her hand and picks a shard of glass out of her palm and brings it to her ear and listens.

Then she scoops a puddle of glass out of the window with her thumb, and plugs her right ear with it, and she listens.

Then she peels a layer of cracking paint from the wood of the door of the closet with the nail of her big toe, and she pulls a scrap of it up to her ear, and she listens.

And then she blows on the carpet until it starts to come apart and a piece of it floats up and up and she catches it with her left ear and she listens.

And then she shakes the things from her ears and walks back to the mattress and puts her mouth to the foot of the bed and sucks out the moisture until her mouth is full of it and spits it into her palm and brings her head down to her hand and she listens.

Then she shakes the liquid from her skin and her fingers and she puts both hands over her ears and listens.

And then the woman gets back into bed, and pulls the covers to her shoulders. She reaches for the phone and picks up the receiver and dials the number of the one who has just whispered to her from the fragments of her bedroom, and she waits for him to pick up so that she can change his weather.

2.

We are watching a man in bed.

There's a telephone on the bedside table, and he sits naked under the covers and he waits.

The phone rings.

He starts, and as he picks up the receiver he can see the room changing: a long crack forms in the wall to his right, and the glass shatters out of the window to his left, and a hole opens up in the ceiling above him as the plaster closes in on itself, and the floor starts to shake, and though his body is being thrown back and forth on the bed he manages to reach across to the table and replace the receiver on the cradle of the phone and the shaking stops.

He pushes the blankets away and gets up and surveys his room. He puts one ear to the crack in the wall, and then walks across the room and puts the other to the glassless window, and then he climbs onto the bed and jumps and jumps until he gets high enough to put his head through the hole in the ceiling, and each time he listens to the pop and crackle and stumble of the voices of broken things.

And then the man falls back into bed and pulls the covers to his neck. He picks up the phone and listens for the dial tone and presses the numbers of the woman who has just surprised him, and he waits for her so that he can surprise her, too.

3.

We are watching a woman in bed who does not like to be surprised.

There's still a telephone on the bedside table, and still she sits naked under the covers and she waits but she does not remember what she is waiting for, so maybe she is not really waiting at all.

The phone rings.

She cannot hear it, but as the weather of her room changes, so does she: the red and the blue of her heart turn silver, and the pink of her skin turns green, and the breath in her lungs turns yellow, and black of her eyes turns white and the whites turn black and her lips go yellow as the breath escapes her as she tries to listen to the colors as they change inside of her but the message is too much, and the phone stops, and so does she.

4.

We are watching a man in bed.

There's a telephone on the bedside table, and he sits naked under the covers and he waits.

But the phone does not ring.

THE GESTURE OF
TELEPHONING

I knew the old man about a year or so before he died. This was over twenty years ago now. Everyone in the neighborhood understood who you were talking about if you mentioned "the old man," even though there were no shortage of retirees in the area. I suppose that was due to his relative wealth, and his eccentric nature. He fully embraced the "old man" archetype, with his horn-rimmed spectacles, shock of white, wiry hair, and formal tweeds of every shade spanning the tan and brown spectrum. I was not able to ascertain his previous line of work, or the source of his income, but I certainly benefitted from the latter. There were rumors that he was once an avant-garde opera singer, but if so, that could not account for his material comforts. The old man was not unfriendly, but he rarely strayed from his rambling house at the end of the cul-de-sac, choked by wisteria, except to feed his cat on the porch, pick up the newspaper waiting for him in the front garden, or accept a delivery. It was exclusively in the mode of the latter that I would interact with him: bringing old telephones, that I had foraged from all over the city, like some kind of improvised currency. I was around thirteen years old at the time, and moved around my suburban world on bicycle wheels far more than on my own two feet. When I discovered, from a small index card pinned to the community bulletin board at the front of our humble supermarket, that the old man would pay cash for old telephones, I saw an opportunity to supplement my allowance without too much effort. First I scoured the pawn shops and thrift stores. When that well ran dry I did some research and discovered a series of offices, past the outer-ring highway, that had been abandoned, but never cleared out. The front door was not even locked. Given that I was limited to pedal-powered transport, I could only deliver what could fit in my backpack at any one time, and I covered many miles that year, riding around town with what sometimes felt like a second person clinging to my back.

Strangely, the old man was not concerned with how rare or vintage any specific telephone was, and paid the same rate for my motley haul: one dollar per phone, no matter the type, age, or model. I would unpack the contents of my bag onto his large dining room table, which was always covered in sheets, and upon which dozens of telephones — at different levels of disassembly or repair — were strewn and piled. He would then stand over my offerings, training a strong light upon the pile, as if about to interrogate them. Indeed, he would poke and prod them with an ornate chopstick, and take little hieroglyphic notes in a small pocket-book produced from inside his waist-coat. Had there been a witness to this little ceremony, they would no doubt recognize a gesture spanning back to the very beginning of human commerce: whether the objects under scrutiny were fish, grapefruit, glassware, or gold. I was fascinated by the ad-hoc communication technology museum all around me, but also felt uncomfortable about lingering there; and was always relieved to return to the sunlight, and my bike, with enough money in my pocket to buy a stash of comics to last all weekend.

Thinking back, it is evident the old man was suffering some kind of monomania. But at the time I just considered him to be an enthusiast, in the same sense that I myself collected base-ball cards, or my mother collected sentimental figurines. This obsession, however, took over every surface of the old man's rambling two-story warren. The lighting was always gloomy and insufficient, except where he had installed his various improvised worktables, so the impression regarding this inventory of telephonic objects was of many waiting *presences,* outside the perimeter of the lamps. Taken as a swarm, paused in mid-gathering, or one by one, as solitary prisoners, they suggested a type of dormant life, coiled tightly inside themselves with the potential to suddenly call out in a clamor. And so, despite the reigning silence, tension filled up the spaces, as if each phone comprised part of a vast alarm system, poised on a hair trigger. While waiting for the old man to go through his inspection ritual, my ears would tingle at the silence of all these plastic creatures, tumbled into a new muteness — waiting, waiting — for the opportunity to initiate a mating call with one of their own kind, between the kitchen and the study, or the bedroom and the bathroom. But I never heard such a sound when I was there. Only the false alarm of the grandfather clock, on the hour and half hour.

Most of the telephones were the classic rotary desk style of the time, with a smattering of the new digital touch-tone ones that were beginning to appear in the cities. Rows and rows of the former were jammed next to each other like commuters; some with their receivers swapped with their neighbor: a somewhat obscene display of promiscuity, perhaps even against their will. So many filled the downstairs bathtub that they created a mountain up towards the ceiling, seemingly ready to topple at any moment. Amidst all the chaos, there were sections of great geometric attention; as if, in a fit of great focus, the old man arranged phones by size or color into Aztec-inspired patterns. Much of the collection was reminiscent of an old European cabinet of curiosities, caring little for scientific taxonomies, and preferring to focus on suggestive resemblances or coincidental affinities. Looking left, I felt a sense of the future of human speech, stretching across the globe into the uncolonized twenty-first century. Looking right, I felt I was the lone visitor at an exhibit proclaiming the archaic, almost paleolithic character, of our technical extensions. Was the old man an archeologist or a prophetic engineer? This question only came to me long after he passed away, but at the time I could feel it forming in my cloudy teenaged brain.

On one occasion, while the old man went to fetch a few extra dollars, I ventured to lift the receiver of a phone sprouting randomly from the wall, surrounded by dozens of its own kind. I was surprised to hear a dial tone. Indeed, at the time — feeling something like a trespasser in this claustrophobic and dreamlike space — the tone sounded more like the telephone's own voice, than a neutral signal awaiting further input. I had the distinct impression this mournful machine was taking the opportunity to give me an account of its overall well-being, or lack of, and I hung up swiftly, in order to be free of its electric lament.

The following week, the old man was feeling more talkative than usual, and invited me on a tour of the rest of the house. One guest room appeared to be some kind of mechanical forest, with dozens of phones glued to the ceiling, so that their receivers dangled down like a thicket of rubber vines, bouncing a little on their coils, the receivers clacking together in the light breeze which eddied around the ever-drafty house. We paused in the dining room, one wall of which had been converted into a large, home-made switchboard. The old man contemplated the zigzag of wires for a while, and then made some slow, manual adjustments, as if playing a new form of chess with an unseen, perhaps omnipotent, opponent.

This must have been when I noticed a rare space cleared for non-telephonic objects on the mantel piece, including a black-and-white photograph of a handsome young man, dressed in a poet's silk shirt, standing in the middle of what appeared to be a spartan rehearsal room. He held a folded script in one hand, and was gesturing with the other; half dramatically, and half in jest. An attractive young woman, with long straight black hair, and draped in a long white dress with wide sleeves, was enjoying the role of addressee, earnestly attempting to stay in character. The camera had captured her just at the moment her lips were starting to break into an unauthorized smile. A bald and bespectacled man in the background, somewhat out of focus, was watching the young pair with an expression blending envy, pride, and amusement. His body language, one hand on hip, gave the impression that he felt himself to be the last bulwark between discipline and anarchy.

Stepping out into the garden, I soon realized that the old man's obsession was not confined to the walls of his house, but also sprawled all the way to the back fence. Telephones of all types were distributed around the place, from the rockery to the haphazard vegetable run. Some stood solitary, like cheerless garden gnomes. Others clustered together, such as the patch of old 1930's phones, buried in such a way that the receivers pushed their way up through the soil like machinic daffodils, some still filled with water from recent rain, or a snail here and there.

I recall saying something typically stupid for an adolescent boy: the first thing beyond half-hearted attempts at haggling, or providing information about the sources of my merchandise. It was something along the lines of, "Wow. Look at all this? I guess you must really like telephones."

I remember the old man's expression in response, down to his last wrinkle and eyebrow bristle. He looked in my direction for a while, staring right through me, as if listening for an echo beneath or inside my own voice (which was cracking between child and adult, untroubled by any real sense of time's passage). He then frowned, as his eyes began to focus on the present again, and I saw his hand falter a little, as it reached for the back of a metal garden chair nearby.

"No no," he replied. "That's not really it. Phones are no more or less important than anything else. I'm just expecting a call, and I want to be sure not to miss it."

I, of course, wanted to ask for more details. But something about his manner discouraged further questioning in that direction, and I followed him back into the house.

As I have already indicated, the old man died a year later. The local paper dedicated three pages of text and photographs to the unwitting museum and makeshift sculpture park that he left behind. I believe an expert from Bell Laboratories came by, in case there was anything of interest, as well as a few curious curators, local historians, and other assorted vultures of the cultural persuasion.

As for me, I took the news with a shrug at the time. But today I find myself thinking about the old man on a regular basis, as I start to understand what it means to be his age, and perhaps even his temperament.

I have only one telephone myself. But I sometimes like to imagine that if I hit upon the right combination, I could hear him once again, croaking *hello* from the other side.

THE GESTURE OF
VIDEO

A bed no longer raises any such questions.
— Flusser, *Gestures,* 142

It is a place on which to sleep, under which to store suitcases, and in which to hide money.

It is a place on which to trace dream fragments in strange alphabets, to sketch lipstick nets on your pillow that will catch and kiss your hair while you sleep, to lay on a bed-sized mirror and stare yourself in the face as you drift into a cold glass slumber and then to wake up and press your skin against the glass and watch the skin stiffen into a silver shell that you can crack and peel off your meat like a hard-boiled egg and take little bites of your knee your forearm your finger and swallow and watch them lump across your body and go right back to where they started, to stand on one leg and shout in the voices of broken things crack! sizzle! crash! rip! and watch as the voices echo in the room around you paper peeling from the walls paint shattering bits of fiber shocked into flames.

It is a place under which to store dog bones love notes lovers fruit pits angels boots, spare fingers and toes as they're shed to grow new ones, spare cats and hamsters, boxes of broken glass, chunks of granite encased in cocoons they've spun around themselves in which they soften and grow into small statues with small mouths that quicken and yawn and bite their way out and crawl up and up and into bed and under the covers and onto your shoulders to sing you small stony lullabies, old shirts full of holes where worms have eaten the fabric and grown wings made of lace and silk and velvet, lizards that change color when you play music for them, lightbulbs you keep under the covers and whisper jokes to so that you can watch them glow as they giggle.

The bed is a place in which to hide secrets, quieting it by feeding it pomegranate seeds under the sheets until the mattress turns red and sour and sated and the bed falls asleep dreaming of autumn and keeping confidences, to hide doors and tunnels and snowmen and crumpled tissues, to hide in the blankets with socks and a flashlight and a map showing gestures made only with hands and wrists and arms and feet and ankles carefully drawn that you study for hours and hours and hours until you learn the pattern and dance it under the covers and wake up as a drawing of a child on the cave walls of Lascaux.

It is a place that makes people in one or two dimensions, direction and surface, line and plane, on and under and in, and it creaks and waits and watches us obey.

The Gesture of
Video

Dr. Lopa Mookerjee blinked away her fatigue, and stared at the screen with frowning attention; the light from the monitor reflected in her black-framed glasses. Every twenty seconds or so, she would make adjustments with the keyboard or mouse, and then her large black pupils would adjust to what the refreshed image revealed to her. A pencil tucked behind her ear seemed to be more a tool for pointing and tracing in meditative speculation than an implement for writing; a fluid and unconscious gesture she made whenever a colleague approached her workstation. Lopa's sleep patterns — never what she or her husband would have wanted — were one of the first things to be impacted further by the recent discoveries. Discoveries that she herself, along with her team, had made, but not yet officially announced to the wider world.

The image on the screen appeared to be some kind of monster, perhaps a movie-still from an old 1950's Hollywood horror film: half malevolent insect, half mutated bird. The creature could conceivably be something a disturbed child might assemble for itself, locked away in a Victorian insane asylum, and obliged to forge its own bed-time companion out of grey felt, black buttons, yellowing leather, and bits of shattered ceramic, porous bone, or bristling bamboo. Lopa clicked a new viewing option from a drop-down menu, and a different monster appeared; this one a vibrant and toxic green, apparently a hybrid of caterpillar and cactus. Rose-like thorns emerged from its rough mossy-textured surface, along with a cluster of talons, surrounding what was presumably a mouth, the shape and color of claw-tipped ginger root.

Lopa confronted these monstrous portraits without any sign of revulsion. Indeed, she had learned to find a certain fondness for them, now that the world's most powerful electron microscope, Horus IV — of which she was in charge — had revealed them to her, in all their miraculous, diverse grotesquerie. Along with her immediate colleagues and assistants, Lopa was initially speechless at the detail provided by this new optical technology. These images were both repulsive and comic. But now she was preoccupied by bigger questions than morphology, at an unprecedented miniscule scale. Something about the bristling undeniability of their bodies suggested both the integrity, vision, and limits of whatever created them. The "intelligent design" in evidence here conveyed the impression that each specimen had been left behind by a talented Edwardian costume designer, fond of Hieronymus Bosch and working with a feverish ingenuity, but hampered by a restricted budget. Pink brain sponges sprouted a forest of serrated black spines. Bright blue figures resembling an elongated praying mantis boasted elaborate helmets of indigo slime. Ant-like creatures replaced their own face with the fanned-out fungus of what looked like shredded books. A fat caramel slug, draped in a tattered mink cape, tapered into a cross-eyed vampiric rooster. Lopa thought of them as her charges now, complete with nicknames inspired by their singular characteristics.

Indeed, this gallery of grotesques reminded Lopa of something Freud had once observed: that even in our dreams, or highest flights of fancy, we cannot imagine something wholly new or alien. That is to say, we are limited to hybrids, chimeras, and crossbreeds, since we cannot see beyond the horizon of terrestrial biological forms. In the case of these monsters, however, magnified several hundred thousands of times their actual size, the forms originated from beyond both the terrestrial and the biological spheres. And yet they were still legible as living bodies.

Lopa swiveled to her left, in order to open a chatbox in an adjacent screen, on the other side of which was her opposite number, located in the original CERN, below Geneva.

"Are you there, Matteo?"

There was only a short pause before the reply came.

"I am indeed. How are things going over there?"

"Just fine, thank you. Are you seeing this?"

Matteo's words fired back.

"Just a moment. I'm running some numbers. Let me pull up your screen."

There was another pause, and then confirmation of visual connection.

Lopa continued.

"I've been looking at our latest subpopulation."

"Pin 57, yes?"

"Correct. I've focused down to 80 picometers. So far I've found six different species, arranged into about four hundred different choirs."

"And the other MOS?" Matteo asked, referring to microorganisms.

"A dust mite or two, surfing a sea of bacteria. Firmicutes especially."

Lopa had no sense at all from Matteo's blinking cursor that he was suddenly having a highly self-conscious moment: one of those occasions of deep and renewed appreciation for the scientific community in which he was embedded, and its ability to describe the miraculous and profoundly enigmatic in technical terms.

"So we're still in Elohim level, it seems," he typed, without giving an indication of his mini-epiphany.

"Indeed," agreed Lopa, with a hint of frustration. "We've had no luck accessing Seraphim or Hashmallim, let alone Malakim."

When it had been confirmed that the new technology now allowed humans to peer, for the very first time, into an angelic dimension — or the "Metatronic scale," as they decided to call it — Lopa understood that it would be necessary to bring in top-tier theologians from all the major faiths (and indeed, some of the more marginalized ones), in order to coordinate the research project; along with its messaging to the public. Given the historical antagonism between religious faith and the scientific method, she had prepared herself for endless debate, but communication turned out to be less of a challenge than she originally thought. Indeed, everyone was so excited about her team's discovery, that they were humbled into a shared sense of purpose and resolve. Apparently the more our advanced tools afford us access to the hidden structures and populations of the world, the more these two fundamentally human endeavors or instincts seek to reconverge. Both are, after all, engaged in decoding the environment. Both attempt to identify and explain hidden laws. Both strive to figure out our place and role in the universe. And both have a deep interest in the lessons learned through revelation and enlightenment. Truth, it turns out, is a common goal and destination, with more than one pathway.

Lopa would never forget that first meeting, in a crowded conference room in the CERN 2 facility outside São Paolo. Each tribe wore their traditional garb, whether these be robes, white coats, or business suits; and each individual soul signaled the validity of their presence to the others via the laminated ID cards hanging around their necks. The head of the facility, Dr. Musaki, who had studied both particle physics and the history of world philosophy at MIT, was especially qualified to frame the conversation; and did so with reference to Democritus, who had anticipated modern atomic theory by two-and-a-half millennia, and without the benefit of advanced machines. Dr. Musaki then moved to the twelfth-century European Scholastics, who not only perfected the discipline of Western angelology, but introduced subfields, such as "emotionology," which involved speculation concerning the love lives of the angels, especially between ranks. Dr. Musaki then made reference to Raqib and Atid, the two recording angels known as *kiraman katibin,* who are said to make detailed note of each of our thoughts and acts, placing them in either the column leading to salvation, or the one leading to damnation. Indeed, he somehow managed to make at least passing reference to each of the cosmologies represented in the room, without losing collective attention, implicitly suggesting that all the different perspectives present were merely different blossoms on the same branch.

It is true that in follow up meetings there was some debate which tradition should be used for the taxonomic nomenclature, given how many religions talk of angels. (Practically all of them, if we take the definition as "spiritual mediator between worlds.") But even the representatives of Islam were surprisingly sanguine about using the Jewish angelic hierarchy for the phylum, provided the models for the genus were sourced from the Quran.

The consensus seemed to be that physics had reached so far that it had become a positivist form of metaphysics: unifying several scattered projects in the process, and now approaching some kind of Zenith.

Lopa continued to toggle between the image and the data her postdocs were generating in response, so Matteo could see the emerging correlations.

"There's one you haven't seen yet, Matteo. I've been saving it for the right moment."

He replied immediately.

"Stop holding out on me!"

"Ok," she smiled. "Prepare yourself."

She then clicked to the next specimen, a tiny creature which looked a bit like a crimson lizard embryo in utero. It had six sets of silky wings. The top pair sprouted from its neck, and covered its eyes. The bottom pair were curled around its feet, in a tender gesture of auto-affection, while the middle pair were spread in the manner of a yawning bat. In addition to all these appendages of flight, the critter had the arms and hands of a humanoid, albeit with more claw-like fingers.

"Oh. My. God," typed Matteo.

"I know," replied Lopa. "Can you believe it?"

"Is that what I think it is?"

"It can't be anything else, right?"

Lopa used her pencil to point to the object which had astonished them so, even though Matteo was on the other side of the world. The graphite tip circled this angel's jealous hands, in which was clutched a golden trumpet, the mouth piece never far from its sleeping mouth.

"Incredible," he wrote back, eventually; all the adrenaline and shock of the last few weeks distilled into one word. "I know I say this every time," he eventually continued, "but I still can't believe we are *actually* counting how many angels are on the head of a pin."

Lopa smiled, also incapable of fully assimilating this new and disorienting reality into her understanding of who she is as a scientist, and — beyond that — as a being among other beings, most of which are invisible to the human eye. She wondered what Plato or Aristotle might have discovered, and deduced, if they had access to even a rudimentary nineteenth-century microscope; let alone this exquisite instrument, extending deep underground, which had taken more than a decade, and several fortunes, to build. The Horus IV, named in honor of the Egyptian falcon-headed sky god — he of the all-seeing eye — captured reality on registers that now began to call reality itself into question. Particle physics was a branch of the sciences that seemed to presume that the Euclidean world had been smashed into atoms. And yet here she was, an Indian-American woman who grew up in New Jersey, unexpectedly patching it back together again; albeit in ways that would make Newton, Einstein, and Feynman scratch their heads. The original CERN, which she now considered Matteo's shop, thought it had found the "God particle," only to find out it was a false alarm. But unless some highly sophisticated prankster was leaving fake entities on the end of sharp objects for her to find, this was no joke. The proof was undeniable: at the molecular level, numinous beings shared para-quantum spaces with dust mites, fungal spores, cyanobacteria, and viruses. The choral-structure of their appearance, along with the eerie songs of eternal praise, captured by the ComCAT acoustical imaging systems, put this beyond a shadow of a doubt. And even as the angels looked closer to demons than the cherubs of medieval oil paintings, they seemed to exhibit the kinds of behaviors described in all the holy writings of the world.

Lopa had always been a staunch atheist, and became impatient with colleagues who believed there was a divine being behind the design of the universe. Somehow the discovery of angels did not shake this atheism, but enlarged it, to now — paradoxically — include the sacred. After all, Spinoza argued for the immanence of a unified substance, in all its temporary manifestations. Whether we call this substance God or not was not as important to Lopa as taking a census of its incarnations. The fact that some actual, verifiable beings are theologically derived was a new conundrum to her: a new paradigm shift, certainly, but not necessarily a shattering of her worldview.

So, God exists after all. Then again, as the debates raged in the corridors around her, is the existence of angels absolute proof of God? Perhaps these spirits are but Divine residues. Until Matteo captured a face in a Higgs boson, she was not going to drop to her knees and pray. Instead, she ate cereal at home in her pajamas, watching loop after loop of video footage of these angels, while her husband snored in the next room; to the extent where her fitful dreams were full of them. Staring into the screen, she sometimes felt like a female Narcissus, captivated by the grotesque reflection in front of her; radically alien, and yet somehow expressing a secret affiliation. A new way of being-in-the-world.

Dr. Lopa Mookerjee, living underneath a volcano like some kind of fairy tale princess, in proud possession of the world's largest magnifying glass. Or like Alice, stepping through the mirror.

"Hello? Are you still there? Geneva to São Paolo? Do you read me?"

Matteo's message shook her out from this latest insomniacal reverie.

"Sorry. Yes, I'm here," she typed in response. "It's true. We are counting angels on the head of a pin."

"Time to hedge my bets," wrote Matteo. "I'm genuflecting in between equations."

"Well," noted Lopa, getting ready to call it a night, and trade her lab coat for pajamas once more. "If history is anything to go by, this isn't the settling of anything, but rather the beginning of ever-more hair-splitting arguments."

"Too true," confirmed Matteo. "For instance, you claim that on the head of Pin 49, a standard one-inch safety pin, you identified a total of 498 angels. My calculations have you short by at least a dozen!"

"Impossible," Lopa replied, smiling. "You couldn't count beer bottles on a wall."

"I'll drink to that," wrote Matteo, known for his fondness for a pint or three.

After signing off, Lopa checked for her keys and her phone, and then reached to switch off the monitor. The lizard-angel shifted in its slumber, and she hesitated a moment, as it brought the trumpet to its lips. Her breath caught in her lungs, and her heart skipped a beat, as she watched this creature's leathery lips and little sharp teeth prepare themselves. But instead of blowing, it just sucked the mouthpiece like a nipple for a while, and then spit it out again, in the midst of an unpleasant dream.

Exhaling deeply in relief, she turned off the monitor, and headed to the parking bay.

THE GESTURE OF
SEARCHING

There is just a woman, and a road and four things: a measuring tape, a stopwatch, a pencil, and a notebook.

She walks. She walks, and looks around, and she stops occasionally to lay down her tape or to stretch it above her or alongside her and take a reading, or to press the button of her watch and wait and press it once again, and take a reading.

She has been doing this for as long as she can remember. She has never met another, although she suspects that others exist.

The road is dry, and it's windy, and sometimes she smells what should be a plant alongside the road, and sometimes she hears what should be a bird in the sky overhead, and sometimes she feels what should be a raindrop on her skin, but she does not know how to see a plant, or hear a bird, or feel a raindrop. In the language that she knows, there is no word for plant, or bird, or raindrop. There are no words for she or her, for I or you, for road, or wind, or walking. No word for self, or other. Her language describes only kinds of proximity, ways of being close or far. Those, she sees and knows and feels and tastes. Those, she records in her notebook, because she is the lexicographer, and it is her job to language kinds of distance.

The word for the intensity of the translucent green of a leaf when it's place atop another.

The word for the sound of the feathers of a wing brushing against the dirt.

The feeling of a raindrop sliding down your cheek.

The gentle pressure of chestskin against wool when inhaling on a cold day.

The time between wishing and forgetting the wish, the length of a sniffle, the span between the parts of her body she could wiggle, between kissing and being kissed, the time it took the pink of a pinch to fade, the time between cut and bleed.

She recorded each of these as a number, filling the pages of her book with them, each naming a kind of distance. The pages held a mathematical language of desire.

There were homophones in her book. The same number marked the length of a certain glance on a certain day, and the distance between two bits of eggshell on the road. The imagined heat of an imagined lover's breath on her hand was equal to the time it took to scrawl that imagined lover's imagined name in the dust.

Each night, she scans the pages of that day's labors and she makes note of these synonyms, for whomever might come after, for whomever she might teach to speak this language, for whomever might care to learn.

But now, we watch as she records the final number on the final page of her notebook, and closes the cover, and sits in the middle of the road.

We watch as she opens the book again, turns to the first line of the first page, picks up a stick, and commences adding in the dirt.

4306. 3. 65. 81. 3490. 2.

We do not keep track of how long she sits and adds. We simply sit, and wait, and watch.

When she is done, when she has summed all of the numbers — all of the words in her language, all of the many names of desire — we watch as she scrawls a single number in the dirt.

She stands and reads the number aloud.

And as she does, we watch as the outline of her begins to blur, the sky becomes visible through her skin, the wind moans through the thin spaces where parts of her used to be. And once she is gone (she did not know we were here, she did not know we had heard her), we go to her book, and we pick it up, and we open the pages, and we begin to read from it.

8. 95. 12849. 600. 12.

As we speak each name, a world of sensation opens up around us, in us, and we gradually learn her language, and we come to understand that she has become that language, too. The more we speak, the less we know who we are, and the more we can feel each other, and can feel her arms reaching out to gather us close and help us joyfully unlearn.

The Gesture of Searching

Two minutes late today. Five minutes late yesterday. And three minutes late the day before that. Which makes ten minutes late in total this week so far. The bosses will not like that. At least, not the city bosses. The managers who sit between these frowning men and myself will take the heat; even though it's never really their fault. The further down the line you get — which, not coincidentally, means the further you get from the city — the less people worry about that sort of thing. Here in the country, people prefer the train to be a bit late. It gives them more time to prepare for the journey, speaking practically, like packing, or mentally, in terms of getting all one's thoughts together, before stepping on board. I suspect that the drivers understand this, and slow down a little, once they pass through the second or third valley. They may lose a bonus here or there. But nobody drives trains purely for the money. There is a fellowship that springs up along the railways, stitched together by the tracks: each train reinforcing the bond, like a giant, steam-powered zipper. After working four years on this humble platform — four years in human time, which I'm obliged to work under; twenty-eight years according to my own body clock — I know every driver's name, every conductor's name, and every signalman's name; and also the names of many of their children. Because of my special status, railway employees make a point of stopping here and introducing themselves. I suppose because I'm so quiet and obedient they find my presence soothing. They open up to me, in ways they wouldn't normally so quickly. That was my experience for the first two years at least. But now the novelty has worn off, and people are more used to a canine stationmaster, they wave and smile, but don't go out of their way to get to know me (or rather, give me the opportunity to know them). For my life isn't terribly complicated. I rise at dawn in summer, or two hours before in winter, and conduct an inspection. I make sure the cleaner did her job in the evening, and that the waiting room is free of all rubbish, and that the grate is filled with firewood, or the fans are already on, depending on the season. I make sure the washrooms are not dirty, and that there is plenty of paper for the customers. I then go to my office, where I listen to the railway radio for any news of problems in the network. If all is well, they play slow big-band jazz classics, which I have learned to like (even as they made me howl in the beginning). At 8am, I make my way to the large megaphone which blossoms over the main door of Platform 1, like a steel orchid. From its rusting throat a metallic voice provides instruction for a ten-minute exercise routine, around which I am obliged to improvise, because the choreography involved was designed for humans, and not for the dozen or so dogs like myself, dotted around the network. (I was only the second dog to be employed by the Company here in Japan; and I like to think I have been doing such a good job that they felt confident in employing the others.) I bark my company pledge at the end of the exercise, and then return to the office, to communicate via telegraph with the signalmen down the track, who will have much more accurate information about my own line. A telephone, specially designed for my species, is also available to talk with other station masters along this particular route, which stretches approximately North–South from Mount Hiba to Yonago. (Obviously I cannot talk to the other stationmasters in their own language, but they have learned my different barks or whimpers to match the limited set of possibilities around our various tasks.) On a normal weekday, I have six trains to shepherd on their way North or South, three in each direction. (This is excluding the two express trains which rumble through my day like angry dragons, and for which I must make sure there are no unsupervised children, or confused grandparents, ready to totter across the tracks.) Once my morning duties have been fulfilled to my satisfaction, I take a few laps of water from the bowl near the side of the station, below the tap (for this is thirsty work), and then take an enjoyable fifteen minutes to gnaw on the soup bones and random gristle which the owner of the nearby ramen stall brings for me, without fail, on his way to work. When the first train arrives, heading North, scheduled for 9.28am, I am back on the platform, ensuring that all visitors to the village have disembarked safely, before giving the signal to the driver that all is well to continue the journey. Our station is so small that only one human works here during the day — Kazumi — an old widow who sells tickets, as well as overly salty snacks that she makes in the evening. At the beginning of my time here we were very close, but over the years we found ourselves with less and less inclination to communicate, so have since drifted into a friendly kind of respect for each other's spaces and silences. On festival days, however, Kazumi will give me a special treat, and tie a colorful ribbon on my collar. A series of different buzzing bells alert me to the progress of trains as they approach the station, but I don't need them once they get to Aokakiyama. I can smell them. And once the passengers arrive, gathering like small flocks of birds on my platform, counting their luggage, or testing umbrellas, they arrive like a riot of fireworks for my nose; each person a cloud of olfactory information, most of which I am forced to ignore for the sake of keeping my mind on the job. They trail a pungent ribbon behind them, which remains for at least an hour after they depart, depending on the strength of the winds, and the resin density of the nearby pines. These people can be nuisances, especially the teenagers, who want to pull my tail, or take photographs with me when I'm in the middle of dealing with an urgent situation. I will admit that some of the more beautiful young women, or tender-hearted young men, who stoop to admire my coat, paws, eyes, or ears will fill me with a warm glow. But mostly I consider them incidental to my day, even as I sometimes speculate about what brought them to my station specifically, of all the stations in the land. Some appear to be in mourning, returning — too late — to say goodbye to an estranged family member. Some are excited, embarking on some kind of expedition, which they no doubt hope will change their fortunes. Some are anxious, heading towards the nearby boarding school, or nurses training center. Others are distracted or suspicious, involved in shady business. Thankfully I have only been obliged to alert the police on one occasion, due to a middle-aged couple who appeared respectable, but I could smell their intentions. They were stealing purses from the waiting room. I cornered and barked at them until the sergeant came, wheezing out of breath, red-faced at the prospect of using his new handcuffs. Not all the passengers are humans, however. Some lapdogs accompany their owners, of course, but I don't have the time of day for these freeloaders. Occasionally I will steal a glance out of curiosity, but then I feel a flash of disgust in my stomach when I see their stupefied faces, fattened or flattened by their idle and meaningless lives, too lazy to even hold their tongues inside their closed mouths. There is one true dog I see on a regular basis, who rides up and down this line as part of a research project regarding his family. Our conversations were amiable enough at the beginning, but once we discovered that we both shared the same partner, perhaps even at the same time, things became a little strained. We still nod to each other when we cross paths. And we will even share a few stilted words about the weather, if the train is late. It seems rude to do otherwise. My closest friend, however, is Koichi. Koichi is a crow, blessed with the famous crow sense of irony. Koichi is something of a philosopher, and fills my head with all sorts of insightful observations, which I promptly forget when I hear a bell from the signalman, or a passenger needs to check the Lost & Found. Koichi has great contempt for the humans, which I secretly enjoy, even as I don't share in this particular investment. He calls them "swarming shell creatures," since they scurry between moving shells and stationary ones, rarely spending time in the Open. (And when they do, they cover themselves in soft shells, so as not to burn, or feel panic from exposure.) Koichi scavenges cigarettes from the waiting room, which he offers me every time, even as I have not once accepted. "Stupid humans," he would mutter, sometimes with sake on his breath. "They jump on and off these racing shells. They puff smoke into the air to move faster than they are supposed to go. They are always in a hurry." "Not always," I counter, for the sake of conversation. "My customers can be very patient when need be." Koichi would scowl: "No no. Always moving; unless they are forced to slow down because the shell-snake is late. That is so rare they build a special space for it. *Waiting Room.* They hate to be in one place for more than a minute, unless they are eating or copulating. They suffer from boredom, which is really just a form of blind-ness." I often chuckle at such portraits of my masters, as I can see the truth in them, even if for me the knowledge has no sting or lesson. Koichi continues undaunted, however: "And blindly they search for the next moment, which lies around the corner. They do not understand that life has no direction. It radiates outward, like ripples in a pool. Time only becomes an arrow if you build giant bows, and launch missiles weighted with feathery futures." Koichi's poetic turns of phrase keep my mind as active as the megaphone voice does for my body. "But Koichi," I respond, "do you not look forward to summer? Do you not anticipate your next meal or cigarette — just as I sit suspended until the next train arrives?" To this he sharpens his beak on the ground in exaggerated consternation. "Nonsense, canine. You understand nothing: sniffing with your ears and listening with your nose. In any case, you have spent so much time in proximity to these ar-rogant creatures that their blindness rubs off on you. I have seen you in the grip of boredom, during blackouts or strikes. You chase your own tail for want of a task." To this I first shrug, since I know he prefers a jaded monologue over spirited debate, be-fore adding: "The humans are restless, it is true. They are forever searching for something, which lies over not only my horizon, but seemingly theirs." "Precisely!" caws Koichi. "They grope into this imaginary space called *tomorrow*, with their hands and blind eyes. They hide in shells, but then send such shells into the sky, across the sea. No doubt they will build train tracks to the moon soon enough. But what are they searching for?" To this I merely blink and wait, guessing the answer from so many similar conversations. "Aaaahhh," Koichi says. "You take me for a two-bit sage. You think I am going to say 'themselves,' as if this were some great revelation. But no, they search for an *escape* from themselves. They envy us our ability to lead an unsearching existence, beyond the bare necessities of life. And so they seek the origins of their driven nature. They suspect that the secret of their restlessness is hidden in the place where it began: their ridiculous 'humanity.' Clearly these shell creatures are lost monkeys, and they want to take the rest of us with them." I nod, persuaded by Koichi's words more than I care to admit, as he continues. "They think they scare my kind with those absurd scarecrows. Those effigies to their own spiritual inertia. When the most frightening thing is when a human arrives with measuring tools and clipboards. My blood goes cold when they measure and point and plan. You don't remember how beautiful this area was before the puffing shell-snakes came. My ancestors keep detailed records, which they sing to us as children. I have played in this landscape before the trains, through these songs. If you knew what these forests were like, you would not be so proud of your work, dreaming about your big bonus bone from the Company when you retire." I involuntarily move from a vigilant sitting position to resting my chin on the platform. "Who knows," Koichi concludes. "You may even start smoking, like me." Together we would always reach such impasses, and then share a silence together that meant more to me than all his clever and bitter words. Then, eventually, when we could hear the signals warning traffic of an oncoming train a mile away, I would remember that I was master of this station, nod my parting respects to my friend, and prepare for another freight of these intriguing soft shell-creatures: the first to drive a wedge between time and space, before trying to stitch them back together again, as witnessed in the fading timetables, pinned to my office wall.

THE GESTURE OF
LOVING

*[C]omplete absorption in the other without loss of the self,…
exactly this moment is love. At the existential level of love, the
tipping over into another, which makes "I" and "you" into "we" …*
— Flusser, *Gestures,* 51

He sat on a log on the beach in the drizzle and watched the water
fall toward him and pull back out again and he saw that the water had fingers that tried to grip the sand as it was dragged back
into the sea and he saw tendrils in the foam on the sand as the
watery women put their heads and faces down and flung their
hair out to try to reach him, just a little bit, just for a little bit,
before they had to leave again.

He was lonely.

He saw long patterns in the water as it crashed, wet limbs
draped in mermaid plaids and velvets, skipping or crawling or
tangled up hot and sliding, and he heard them speaking watery languages in watery voices, and he scooped a wet bed in
the sand and nestled his seminar copy of Lawrence's *Women
in Love* — his professor, he knew, would understand — and he
covered it over and fashioned a little sandcastle-cocktail-glass

above it and left it as a gift for the mermaids and he got up and brushed the sand from his seat and moved toward dinner.

He came here often. He had buried a little library in the waves, marked with sandcastle-cakes and sandcastle-candles, romantic offerings left for the sea and the women with the foamy hair and the saltwater fingernails. He did not know if he loved them. He did not know, not anymore, what being in love was meant to feel like. And still he went to class, and he came here, and he left gifts for his sandcastle library, and he brushed the sand from his clothes, and he left. He tried to imagine the sea reading stories from his treasured copy of Ovid — he had begun burying the *Metamorphoses* chapter by chapter — between forkfuls of shepherd's pie suppers and sips of gin and tonic.

One late afternoon he came to the beach with his rapidly-deteriorating copy of *Metamorphoses* and thought he might read Ovid's flood story to the waves. As he settled in, however, he glanced to his left and noticed a fairly large structure that had risen from the sand since his last visit. It was a damp sandy slice of a common storefront, a sandcastle-shop fronted by a driftwood sign glued with pink pearls spelling the word "Psychic." Underneath the driftwood was a smaller note attached somehow to the sandy wall above a sandy doorframe: "Madame Gavorski," it said in glue and crushed seashells. "World-Renowned Mentalist. Walk-ins Welcome."

Hanging from the doorframe was a curtain of beads made of tiny single sand grains strung together he knew not how. He waved his hand through it and the beads came unstrung and he closed his eyes and walked through a sheet of falling sand and when he opened them again, eyelashes strung with tiny sandy beads, the curtain had somehow re-formed behind him. It smelled like saltwater and vanilla and fish and musk. Just inside the room, an old woman sat at a small table surrounded by glass objects. To her left was a deck of Tarot cards, and when she held one up he saw sand-beaded eyelashes blinking at him through a pair of delicately painted angel's wings on an impossibly thin sheet of glass. (When she put the card back and shuffled the glass deck, the sandy room was full of crisp glassy tinkling.) To her right was a small crystal ball. In front of her was a teacup full of seaglass and bits of mirror.

She placed a glass card in from of him, face down. And then another, and another.

She wordlessly turned over the first card. Painted on the glass was a woman turning into a tree, and he recognized Daphne from the first of Ovid's stories he had read to the waves.

She turned over the second card, and he saw snakes curling up from the ground and recognized Medusa from the second of Ovid's stories he had read to the waves.

When she turned over the third, he saw the sun and remembered the third story — of the tragic death of Apollo's son — he had read to the waves.

One by one, she placed each glass card on the table. As she turned them over, one by one, he saw that this was a Tarot deck made entirely of The Lovers, each card adorned with a figure from the stories in the pages he had buried in the beach.

She gathered the cards together, and shuffled them again, and placed the deck in front of him.

The stack was no longer glassy and translucent: he saw a delicate pile of the thinnest slivers of pearly turquoise. Madame G. held up three fingers, and Will turned over three cards in sequence. He read across them, and the images began to tell a story.

As his gaze traveled down the first card from top to bottom, he saw a shapely stockinged leg being caressed by a pair of large strong hands.

The second card showed only an open glossy pair of lips and a chin dripping with some sort of dark pink juice.

The third card showed the blurred image of a sheet of paper covered in a curving script scrawled passionately.

In each card he recognized a gesture. Obsession. Desire. Confession.

He looked from the table to Madame G., who looked from his eyes out past the sandy walls and toward the water. He nodded to her, understanding.

As the lonely young man got up to leave the quiet old woman, she handed him a fourth card and closed her eyes and mimed sleep, and he understood that he was to keep this card under his pillow.

When he exited the sandcastle and looked down at the thin flake of blue stone in his hand, he saw that it was The Fool.

Will went home that night and pulled his laptop into bed with him and typed three pages. One page described the tiny feet of the first woman he could remember feeling obsessed with. One page was full of the sensory memory of the restaurant at which he and his second crush lunched before making love for the first time. One page was filled only with punctuation: he had given away all the words he had for his last love, and could now recall only the stops and the pauses and the breaths between declarations. When he was finished, he printed out the pages and placed the Tarot card beneath his pillow and closed his eyes.

When Will woke up the next morning, he gathered the blue dust from the sheets — he had destroyed the delicate card in his sleep — and eased it into a plastic baggie and left his apartment.

He arrived at the beach, opened the bag, and sprinkled the little pieces of pearly blue into the sand around him. And then he settled in, and took out his three printed pages, and began to read the first to the water.

As he intoned tiny phrases about tiny toes and tiny toenails, the surface rippled up in tiny little waves to catch his words and bring them into the water. He got up and moved closer, and as he looked out at the sea he thought he saw a watery woman with webby feet speeding away from a large fish that chased her in hot pursuit. She seemed to be smiling, from what he could see, but it was all over so quickly that he was already losing the image of her kicking legs when he looked down and noticed a blue high-heeled shoe wash up on the sand. He picked it up and turned it over, frowning at the odd finny shape of the toe, and took it back to his blanket, and pulled out the second of his pages and began to read.

The air filled with the smells of cabbage and sausages, and the waves took on the color of mustard, and again he got up and moved closer to the water's edge and looked down into the brown-yellow froth to find two figures with pearls for eyes, a man and a woman, gazing at each other while taking lusty bites out of seashells shaped like apples and marshmallows and then taking bites out of each other before sinking together into the sand in a hot tangled froth. He was still staring after them when something tumbled against his toes, and when he picked it up he marveled at what looked to be a sea-blue strawberry with a bite taken out of it. He took it back to his blanket, and pulled out the third of his pages and began to read.

Here there were no words. Here his voice was silence. But his eyes took the punctuation into his body, and his body brought it into the sand, and the grains became commas and ampersands that made stops and pauses and long asides in the water and again he got up and walked to the edge of the waves but when he looked down, this time, he saw only his own reflection — but no, it was the reflection of a memory of him, and as he looked he thought back to that moment, when he was writing his first love-note to his last love. He was startled from that memory by a sharp prick on his leg, and when he looked down he saw a dribble of blue ink running from his ankle, and when he picked up the offending object he found a long pen made of turquoise. He brought it back to his blanket, and used it to sign the three printed pages — the cartridge was full of sea water — and he took them to the water and gave them to the waves, and he wrapped the shoe and the strawberry and the pen up in his blanket.

As he got ready to leave the beach, he glanced to his left and noticed the familiar sandcastle-storefront with the familiar signage, and he walked over and made his way inside to offer the three sea trinkets to Madame G.

A sheet hung, this time, from the doorframe — it was slick and dark and woven from seaweed and crystalled with salt and he lifted it aside to find a young woman at a small table crawling with crabs. To her left was a broken Tarot deck, and when she held up a misshapen card he saw thin green fronds where her eyelashes should have been, blinking at him through a hole in the opalescent fragment.

To her right was a large clamshell. In front of her was a wine-glass full of pearls.

He did not recognize her.

She put the card down, and lifted the glass, and opened her mouth, and tilted its contents inside. After some sucking and some chewing, she spit a pearly mass onto the table, and kneaded it like dough, and spread it out across the surface, and brought her teeth down to take card-sized bites and spit them out into her hands until the table was clean. She kept her fists clenched around the cards and looked at him, and waited.

He unfolded his blanket and placed his gifts in a row on the table in front of her: the shoe, the strawberry, the pen. She un-clenched one hand and dropped the three cards she had been holding, each in front of one its corresponding objects: Obses-sion. Desire. Confession.

He looked on as she used her free hand to bring shoe, straw-berry, pen, and their matching cards into her mouth, along with a crab or two, and crunched and cracked and squeaked and when she opened her lips to smile at him he saw that she had pearls for teeth and a mussel for a tongue and when she breathed out she made little blue puffs. She opened her other hand and placed three pearly cards face down in front of him and then closed her mouth and stopped smiling and held his gaze.

She put her hand on the first card and looked at him and shook her head. Understanding, he picked it up without turning it over and he gently put it into his pocket.

She then flexed a fingernail and scratched it across the sur-face of the second card, and she brought a finger dazzled in pearl dust to Will's mouth and brushed it against his lips before mov-ing it, in turn, to her own mouth and sucking it clean. Heart nearly beating out of his chest, again he understood, and picked the card up and put it into his pocket.

Watching him watching her, she met his gaze and matched his rapid breathing with her own, in and out over and over until she saw his eyes fluttering — until they both dizzied with the tension — and she scooped the third card off the table and smashed it against the clamshell and closed her eyes. Again he understood, and swept up the shards of the final card and put them into his pocket.

And so, Will left the young woman to seek his next three gestures. Waiting. Seduction. Surrender.

That night he went home and lifted his notebook and a pen into bed and he wrote three pages. On one page, he remembered the way his last lover looked, from across the train station, on the morning when she had come to see him from very far away. On one page he remembered what she smelled like later that day while he was pushing the strap of her dress from her shoulder and leaning in to kiss her neck. He left one page blank, not having the language for what came next. He placed the pages under his pillow, along with the three cards the young woman had given him, and he closed his eyes.

Will woke the next morning — still, his sheets glowed with blue dust — and he pulled the pages from beneath his pillow. When he searched for the cards, his fingers found only three tiny bulges. He swept them out onto the sheets, and saw three small pearls: one in the shape of a brooch, one the smallest of perfume bottles, and one in the shape of a very tiny ear. He scooped them into his pocket and grabbed the pages and brushed his fingers through his hair and left his apartment.

He arrived at the beach, settled in once again, placed the first of the three pages in his lap, and began to read to the water.

As he gave the image of his waiting lover to the sea — brown eyes, cold skin, shivering lip, fingers on suitcase — he saw the seaweed come together, rising to the surface and weaving itself into a velvety green column that fluttered from water to sand and washed up against his feet. He lifted the scarf — just like the one she wore, only salty and speckled with sand — and wrapped it around his neck and shoulders, and pulled out the second page and began to read.

His whole body blushed as he tried his best to tell the sea of the sharp musky smell of warm neck that crawled from his nose to his throat to his fingers as he nudged his lover's silk from her skin and he had only gotten part of the way through when a scent rose from the waves and drenched his skin and settled in his lungs and he kept it there for later.

He took the third blank page from his notebook, and took the three pearls from his pocket, and wrapped them in the paper, and walked to the edge of the water, and Will threw his pearly package as far as he could into the sea. He stood there for some time, thinking about what he might have written on that page, until he felt soft wet salty fingers circling his ankles and pulling him into the water. Unable to resist, Will walked into the waves until they covered his shoulders, and he grasped at his scarf as it came unwound, and he held his breath and closed his eyes as he went under. When will opened his eyes, still submerged, he saw a sandy mound before him, fronted by a sandy door that was hung with a familiar sign. "Psychic," he read in pearls, and when he quickly looked for them he spotted the three that he had given to the water, and he plucked those free and pocketed them while pushing his way through a curtain of suckered tentacles. Once inside, Will found himself standing before a very young girl seated at a table that was covered in the largest octopus he had ever seen. The girl stroked the creature's head with one hand, and with the other she beckoned him closer. He sat, and he breathed in the scent of shiso leaf and plum, and he breathed out the perfume that the sea had given him. The girl swallowed it and nodded and the memory of the scent of the neck of Will's lover crept into her own neck, and as she bent it toward him she gathered the seaweed-scarf from his shoulders and wrapped it around her, and she nodded. Then the girl took her small hand from the octopus and held it out before him, and he took the three pearls from his pocket and placed them in her palm. She fed them to the creature on the table, and she looked up at Will with octopus eyes, and her forehead began to bulge and her skin took on the color of the sand around her and when she opened her mouth he understood that he was to reach inside. And so he did, and from inside of her he pulled a handful of pebbles.

He turned to leave, and threw one of the pebbles in front of him. It grew into a tree whose branches broke through the top of the ceiling. Will climbed them, and when he reached the top — still underwater — he floated another of the pebbles out away from his body. He watched it expand into a balloon, and he jumped into its basket and gulped its air as it rose through the water. Once the balloon had broken the surface, Will tossed the rest of the pebbles into the sea. They grew into an improbable cobblestone path, and he lifted himself onto it and followed it all the way to the shore.

Waiting for Will on the beach was a woman from his seminar. She was reading from his copy of *Women in Love* and sipping from a martini glass that appeared to be made of sand, and when she saw him she smiled and beckoned him over.

They still walk down that beach sometimes, hand in hand. And sometimes, if they're there at just the right time, Will swears to her that he can just make out three figures rising from the sand together in the distance: an old woman made of glass, a young woman made of pearls, and a little girl with an octopus for a head. Sometimes, he whispers to his love, he's sure he sees the women walking toward them. And when he whispers this, she always laughs, and pulls him toward her, and kisses him all over his face. And always, he looks back toward the women made of glass and pearls and tentacles. And always, always, they've gone.

THE GESTURE OF
LOVING

Will sat on a bench in the West section of Washington Square Park, and watched humanity — washed and unwashed — pass him by. They moved at different speeds and with different gaits. They wore different colored and textured fabrics, of different cuts, lengths, silhouettes and degrees of decorum or drama. They spoke in different voices, accents, languages; often trailing dogs as varied as the people thronging along, taking advantage of one of the first weekends auguring Spring. Some representatives of this gentle flow of humanity would slow down, or even stop, when they caught Will's eye, and try to sell him reefer, postcards, Bibles, incense, chap books, chocolate bars, subscriptions, or enlightenment. One older woman, several months earlier, had sat very close to him on the same bench, and appeared to even be offering herself. She had become bashful and left, however, when Will pretended not to understand English.

Today — due to the encouraging weather, no doubt — the mood was light. The sun glinted off the windows of the buildings, which loomed and gathered around the park like watchfully indulgent parents. A jazz band had seemingly sprung out of the soil, like the snowdrops and daffodils which were now beginning to push their cheerful heads sleepily out of the ground.

Will had a cheap second-hand copy of a book in his hands, folded back in the manner of the avid reader who did not, for all that, grow up in a household in which caring for the spinal health of a book was instructed to be a priority. This particular book was a pulp paperback version of D.H. Lawrence's *Women in Love,* and Will was having trouble staying in the story, given the slow cascade of actual women — in love or not — streaming past him. He had three more days to finish the novel before his next class on "Literature and Eros" at the New School, where he was studying on the GI Bill. Two years ago, Lawrence's books had been passed around Will's battalion, thumbed and smudged to the point of unreadability, along with Henry Miller and other less reputable authors, with unrecognizable pseudonyms, yet dealing with highly familiar human themes and foibles. To say these dog-eared artifacts were also inspired by Eros may have been giving them too much credit. Then again, Will's professor seemed openminded enough to consider popular purple prose alongside literary masterpieces. "They are all, let's admit, expressions of love," said his professor, "each as legitimate as the other; just as a rude and hearty village Bolognese is no less an instance of *food* as something sweated over by a chef at the Cordon Bleu." Will enjoyed these classes, even as he became easily distracted by pursuing a thought to its conclusion, tossed playfully to the group by his instructor. Or, just as frequently, he became distracted by the pastel sweater, vibrant neckerchief, or chipped fingernail polish of one of the six young women in the class, all of whom overlapped in his mind, as soon as he left the room.

As a rule, Will preferred not to stare love in the face. His choice in college courses, however, suggested a latent desire to approach this topic as directly as he could manage. He had returned from Korea to find his fiancée married to his high-school rival. And while this stung hard at the time, and soured his feelings on matters of the heart, he was slowly learning — simply through the act of visual exposure to the sheer number of eligible women in the city of New York — that he would be foolish to retire from the game altogether, or to pickle his young heart in a bitter brine. Will was not bad looking, or so he had been told over the years, by people more objective than his mother. Unlike several of his friends, he was lucky enough to have all of his limbs. And the nature of his military postings meant that he had been spared, for the most part, the kind of action which rattles the mind to the point of no return. He even dabbled in poetry, as seemingly every young man living in Greenwich Village did in 1955.

Also, like every young man living in Greenwich Village at this time, he was confused about the line, if there was one, between love and sex. While it was mandatory to talk with his friends about the latter, in the boastful mode, the former was off-limits in normal conversation. Perhaps that's why he felt compelled to take a class on the theme. People have been agonizing with the question of love "since the dawn of time" (a phrase that Will had used in his first assignment in this class, and one which his professor had struck through with a red pen in three firm strokes). And yet it was more of a taboo to discuss the moods and shadows of the heart than the blind gropings of the loins. Several statements, presented simply as fact by his professor (one Dr. Walser), echoed around Will's mind, as he tried to follow the elusive moral of this bold Englishman's novel. The first had struck him with the force of an epiphany: "You can buy sex. But you cannot buy a lover." Having spent several lost weekends in Seoul, Will knew instinctively this to be true. But it was another matter to have it formulated into words by an older gentleman with a sharp goatee, and even sharper intellect.

Other statements had not been so pithy, but Will had scribbled them down in his notebook as best as could, rereading them later, as he tried to tap out an essay on Ovid on his neighbor's borrowed typewriter, until their import wavered, dissolved, and then reconstituted themselves. "In order to approach and understand the social phenomenon of love, we must pay attention to its gestures. For there is no love without *the gesture of loving*. We must therefore invent and utilize a phenomenology of the gesture of loving." Below this short paragraph Will had written four Greek words: *eros, philia, charisma, empathia*. In parentheses he had written two questions to puzzle over himself: "(How to distinguish between love and lust? Do not the gestures often look the same?)" And this was followed by another comment from his professor: "The gesture of loving appears to be a gesture that makes use of sexuality, like the gesture of painting makes use of a brush." This analogy had immediately reminded Will of the occasion, not too long ago, when one of his college-mates had invited him to a painting studio, to view some canvases which had forgone the brush altogether, in favor of "primitivist" body paintings, and images made from blowing pigments directly on to the blank surface.

But such insights seemed rather distant on this fine weekend; watching the parade of people walking by. Loneliness, for Will, had become a closer friend than anyone he had yet met in his classes; to the extent that it felt less like a burden, and more like a wizard's familiar. His attempts at asking the co-eds on a date were clumsy; and the one fish that *had* nibbled, had subsequently stared at him, over garlic bread knots and a red-checkered vinyl tablecloth, as if from the depths of an aquarium, as he tried his best to make an account of himself that didn't sound like it came from a high-school year-book or random obituary. Moreover, he could not tell if reading Wharton, Fitzgerald, Forster, and Lawrence were helping or hindering his comprehension of, and thus ease around, the fair sex. He could feel his brain stuttering whenever he came within the orbit of perfume or pearly smiles. Once, on the subway to Coney Island, a girl from the Bronx winked at him, before striking up a conversation. His hands still started to sweat when he remembered how aloof he acted, until she shrugged and returned to her more timid friend; all the while as the voice inside his head begged this gum-chewing messenger to stay; to go on the roller-coaster with him; and share cotton candy.

Eventually, Will succumbed to the less abstract appetite of hunger in the stomach; tucked the book into his coat pocket, and headed towards the diner nestled directly two floors beneath his apartment. After eating a bowl of hot borscht, and two giant slices of challah toast, Will felt reluctant to return to his sparse student room, and the overfamiliar feelings that awaited him there. Like the rest of the city, the weather seemed to be pulling him by the sleeve, to bid him to stay outside, and remember what it was like to be a public being in public spaces, exposed to the many zephyrs of the multitude. And so he walked West to the water, and watched the boats go by. As the blue began to leach from the sky, Will pulled up his collar against the lingering chill winds of late winter, and relocated to the Ear Inn, where he spent more than he would usually allow himself on a shepherd's pie and two pints of Guinness. Here he had ventured a few tentative words with an attractive young woman, who had clearly been stood up by a date, but who was now putting a brave face on the affair. Will's inability to turn this situation to his advantage began to gnaw at him more than he thought it would, as she bid him a polite thank you and goodbye. Walking home in a mood hovering a shade or two above the gloomy, he passed a window that had become an intimate part of his map of the immediate neighborhood. This window was draped with rather faded curtains, that were once plush, deep-red velvet, cinched in the middle by a gold tassel. Various charms and knick-knacks were strewn about the window display, which featured a red neon sign, outlining the word: "Psychic." A hand-painted sign reading: "Madame Gavorski, World-Renowned Mentalist. Walk-ins Welcome" was hung next to the door, above a rough approximation of an Ankh. Will was familiar with Madame Gavorski herself, as she often sat in the window, knitting or playing solitaire, occasionally pausing to smile both wanly and welcomingly at passers-by. He could not say why it was on this occasion, as opposed to the hundreds of other times that she beckoned him with a half-hearted gesture of solicitation, that he found himself pausing in front of the shop front, and then walking inside.

Madame Gavorski welcomed Will as if this were a weekly ritual, and he felt instantly disarmed by the way she greeted him like family. She ushered her guest through a beaded curtain into a room which smelt heavily of various musks and vanillas, bidding him to sit at a small table, upon which sat the tools of her trade: Tarot cards, tea leaves, even a small crystal ball, which seemed too toy-like to give any clear visions. Will had never looked closely at Madame Gavorski, since he was always anxious to avoid the eye contact which may lead to being in precisely this situation: sitting inside her parlor, and thus obliged to cross her palm with the modern American equivalent of silver. But the glasses of dark beer had clearly given him a stout heart; and he took this opportunity to consider the fortune teller's face; tired as it was, and caked in make-up. Madame Gavorski was of a certain age, agreeably plump, and with smiling eyes that clashed with a rather down-turned mouth. She dressed like a gypsy; and he could not tell if her Romanian accent was real or put on. Strangely, he felt more at ease in this eccentric parlor — with its candles and waxen sigils — than in his own apartment, or in the classroom in which he dreaded being called upon to give a lucid opinion.

"So you finally come to see me," said Madame Gavorski, as if to verify her powers of seduction. "I see you walking back and forth every day. You do your laundry yourself. You do not give it to the Chinaman. I see these things. I see other things too."

"What else do you see?" asked Will, his tongue feeling looser than with the young woman he had spoken to earlier at the bar.

"Patience, my child," chided Madame Gavorski. "I need to get a better sense of your aura before we jump into my Art."

Will nodded, as the psychic squinted her eyes and observed him with a shrewd and penetrating gaze. Sensing the comic aspect of the situation, Will felt remarkably relaxed, as if he was in on some joke, being performed for an invisible audience.

"You were a soldier," she said. "You have seen great suffering."

Will did not reply, suspecting that his posture or haircut gave him away. He wasn't sure if it was the beer, or the one-bar radiator glowing in the corner, but any suffering he had seen at this moment felt remote and muffled.

"But now you seek something," she continued.

"I do?" asked Will, playing his part as best he could.

"Yes, of course! Who is not seeking something?" Madame Gavorski asked, with a mischievous twinkle, eliciting a wry smile from her new client.

"But," she continued, "before I perform a reading, you should tell me how much your donation will be. I can only offer visions in keeping with the compensation." She smiled a very American smile, to acknowledge the economics of the situation. "I'm sure you understand."

Will fished around in his pockets, and produced a ten-dollar bill. This was how he knew himself to be rather intoxicated; since this was enough money to feed himself for a couple of weeks, or to buy two semesters' worth of books. Madame Gavorski's eyes widened in sincere surprise, before continuing. "I see. It appears you seek this thing more urgently than your body language indicates. I can only assume it involves the heart, since a young man like yourself does not need a fortune teller for anything else, unless he is caught up in gambling."

Will briefly considered conjuring up a false story to account for his presence in Madame Gavorski's parlor, but discovered that his tongue was speaking sincerely on his own behalf. "Yes. Yes I suppose that's it. I don't really want to see the future; and I don't really believe that you can see it."

Madame Gavorski batted a false eyelash, but did not break her smile, while Will continued.

"Rather, I need some help. Cosmic help, I guess you might say. Nothing sinister, you see. But surely there are ways a man can get...well...*assistance*...from the elements, to be more... well...attractive. Or persuasive. Or...I don't know...I'm not expressing myself very well."

Madame Gavorski observed the young man in silence for a while, introducing a new note of sympathy between them. She then asked for his hand, and studied the lines on Will's palm with a practiced intensity.

"You are very sensitive," she declared. "You feel deeply; even if you are not gifted at putting these feelings into words." Will winced a little, remembering the poems sitting in a desk drawer, two blocks away. "I see things in your future — good things, and bad things. But you say you do not want to know them, and I always respect my client's wishes on that account."

Will found himself becoming less skeptical by the minute, as Madame Gavorski wove her occultish ways around him.

"If I understand you correctly," she continued, "you are looking for a spell. A potion perhaps." She then smiled in a somewhat lewd manner. "A *love* spell. Or a *love* potion, yes?"

Will felt himself blush, but was also glad that this humble sorceress understood, without obliging him to be more explicit.

"Yes, I suppose so. But not in a way that would go against the woman's wishes, you understand? I don't want to hypnotize anyone into doing something they wouldn't normally want to do. I just want to feel more confident. I want to be able to communicate my interest in a lady without scaring her away." At this, Will started to feel tiny pinpricks in his eyes, and realized he was starting to get misty at himself, and his own lot in life.

Madame Gavorski, a professionally perceptive woman, picked up on this. "I see the sadness in you, young man. But do not be ashamed. After all, to feel sorry for oneself is merely to turn a natural empathy inwards." She placed both her palms against her own ample bosom, and pushed firmly towards her heart.

Will blinked, both touched and confused by these words.

The psychic continued: "I can do what you say. Indeed, I have helped men far less handsome than you; and more shy."

Will felt suddenly buoyed by this declaration, smiled, and sat up straighter in his chair.

"Yes yes," added Madame Gavorski. "You are already a special client. I can see how much this means to you. I do not play games with people. Although…" and here the mentalist's brow made a rather Shakespearean expression, "…I could, of course, if I wanted to."

"How does this work?" asked Will, impatient to hear details.

"Well, this will take two more visits." Will's brow furrowed at this news; to which Madame Gavorski responded, "worry not, young man. Your money here today will cover them all. But you *will* need to bring me several things. In order to work my magic, I need special objects which connect us both to the desired… how shall we say…*fluency* of the heart you seek."

Will frowned once more. "I'm not sure I follow."

"Worry not. Still yourself. I shall give you detailed instructions," the old woman said, fishing in a velvet bag filled with colored stones. She then drew one out of the bag, turquoise, and placed it in the middle of a chessboard, which had been cleared of any pieces. For what felt like several minutes, she moved the stone slowly and deliberately around the board, as if playing a game of checkers with an invisible opponent; muttering under her breath as she did so. Then, as abruptly as she began this little ritual, she looked up at Will, and gave him the stone.

"Here," she said. "Put this under your pillow, and don't remove it until the spell has worked. It will give you strange dreams. No matter."

Will took the stone, and put it in his shirt pocket, continuing to play his part in this little production.

Madame Gavorski continued: "Today I give you three tasks. When you come back, I will give you three more. After these six objects have been obtained, and I can harness their energies, you will have what you seek."

Will nodded, still unclear on the path ahead.

"When you leave here, you will look *not* for a woman to entrance, but for the *gestures* of love."

This word sent a shivering spark of electricity up Will's spine; given how clearly they recalled the terms used in his lectures on Eros.

"Wait, wait," he interjected. "Did you just say the gesture of love?"

"I did indeed."

"But…but, that's very strange. Do you know Professor Walser?"

"I don't believe I have had the pleasure; although, as you may have noticed, the names of my clients are not as important as their spirit, and the direction this spirit is pointed."

Will felt goosebumps tingling over his body; as he struggled to keep his innate incredulity for the supernatural intact.

"That is very strange," he said, distractedly.

"Strange is my *métier*," quipped Madame Gavorski. "Although it does not feel strange to me."

Will suddenly smelled the strong scent of tomato soup, coming from another room.

"As I was saying," continued the old woman, "you must pay attention to the gesture of love, and not to the people under Cupid's influence. Watch what they are doing; how they express their affection. More to the point, I want you to bring me a memento of these gestures."

"A memento?"

"Yes indeed. An object, connected to a loving gesture."

"You mean, you want me to steal?"

"Oh, I wouldn't say that. Borrow perhaps; though it's true you will be unlikely to find an opportunity to return these items. But lovers are so self-involved. They will barely notice. As long as you do not steal their heart, or the object of their passion, they will forgive anything; that is, if they *do* even notice."

Will nodded, following the logic here as far as he could, given that it was designed to help him. Madame Gavorski continued: "As you may or may not know, love is not one big thing. It is not a giant bowl of tomato soup. It is made up of little pieces. Each little piece is a gesture."

Will nodded, absorbed more by this little lecture, than by the ones he attended at The New School.

"Indeed," said Madame Gavorski, leaning forward in a conspiratorial motion, obliging Will to do the same. "I'm going to tell you a secret now. There is no such thing as love."

She raised her penciled eyebrows dramatically; as if to say, "what do you think of *that,* young man? Just like Santa Claus all over again, yes?" She then leaned in again, and continued.

"I'm afraid it's true. There is no such thing as 'love.' There is only *loving.*"

"Again," ventured Will. "I don't think I follow."

"Oh you will, you will. At least I *hope* you will. You see, people think they are either in love, or not in love. As if love is a giant lake, or a club! But love must be *made,* in order to exist. And once it is made, it must keep being made; or else it falls apart. And we make this love through loving gestures."

Will listened intently, both sensing and resisting a deeper truth in these startling claims. "But," he objected, "I could love someone, without showing or telling them."

"Could you?" countered the psychic. "Loving must be shared. Created together.…What you are talking about is a combination of narcissism and obsession. In such a case you make loving gestures only in your own selfish head. This is not love. This is purgatory."

Will had no answer to this assertion. And so Madame Gavorski snapped back into a less philosophical tone, in order to continue with her instructions.

"So, let us start with the gesture of obsession, since that is indeed where the seeds may grow. Also, the gesture of appetite. In addition to this, the gesture of declaration. So to say, monomania on the one hand. And desire on the other. With confession linking these together. The task should be clear, then. Go into this wild city. Beyond these walls, and bring me back three trophies you find: one snatched from an obsessive (or the one obsessed upon), another bearing the mark of great hunger of the heart, and the last being the means of a sincere admission of the smitten."

Will's eyes widened at the prospect of this quest. He also realized he very much needed to pee. And so the young man rather abruptly thanked his new guide, promised to return as soon as he had secured these three objects — objects which would hopefully be charged with enough amorous energy to help soon infuse his own bold gestures of love — and scampered back to his apartment, where he urinated longer than he ever had in his life.

* * *

That night, Will found sleep to be elusive, as the unusual events of the evening tumbled over and over in the warm and suffocating washer-dryer of his mind. He had dutifully put the turquoise stone under his pillow, and could now feel its watchful presence in his newly sensitized consciousness. He lay on his back, eyes tracing the geometric patterns which the street lights threw on to the ceiling. Was he now a crazy person? Or worse, was he now a foolish or pathetic person, trying to use magic to increase his romantic prospects, like a desperate divorcée? Surely he could never tell his friends or family that he was dabbling in the occult in this fashion. And yet, Will had never felt so comfortable as in Madame Gavorski's parlor. And he had never been so persuaded by the pearls of wisdom of another. While Will had not yet been married, nor held a mortgage, he had flown in a helicopter over burning villages, and seen a prisoner-of-war swinging from the ceiling in a noose made of bed-sheets. This entitled him to feel somewhat of a worldly soul. And yet there was something deep in his bones that felt anything but. Was it wise to trust in powers that, after all, most cultures had throughout history put some faith in? Or was it a sign of soft-headednes?

Either way, Will had spent ten dollars on this wager with the universe. And truth be told, he enjoyed having tasks to complete that did not involve understanding the indirect free mode of literary address or the re-heating of his own canned soup. He also enjoyed playing spy, now that his actual days of stalking his fellow man were over (and now that he could do so with decidedly less stakes involved). And so the young man resolved to see this folly through, whether it was based on sound cosmic principles, or the kitsch and practiced whim of a middle-aged Eastern European woman; promptly falling sound asleep, once he did so.

The next day, Will tried to finish *Women in Love,* but grew restless with the bloodlessness of ink on paper, when real plasma-flushed ladies were involved in loving gestures all over the city, just outside his door. An uncommon thick bank of fog had rolled in over Manhattan, as fresh cold air met the warm residues of yesterday. Will decided to stuff the book unceremoniously between two others — abandoning and suspending the male protagonists in the midst of their fireside homoerotic wrestling match — and throw on his coat once more, buttoned up to the neck on this occasion. But where to go? It was too cold to sit in the park for very long.

And so, Will found himself walking north along Fifth Avenue, taking in the sights, sounds, and smells of the city as if through new pupils, eardrums, and nostrils. Something about his new quest sharpened and focused Will's senses. He was on the hunt for something both specific and vague: gestures of loving. A business man across the road, flagging down a cab, caught his eye, since this was certainly a gesture. But it lacked the requisite passion he was looking for. And so he walked on; his eyes darting from person to person, looking specifically for couples. Most people, however, seemed to be involved more in civic commerce than sensual congress. Will passed an idle fire truck, filled with blue-collar masculinity, smoldering like the embers they had perhaps recently proclaimed safe. Some loud cat calls came from therein, as two women in woolen skirts walked by, feigning not to hear the din. Will continued on, since there was no heart to be found in such a scene.

It felt good to walk, and Will realized just how much he had been cooped up in his apartment, or within the college grounds, during the seemingly endless gray corridors of winter. He continued up into Broadway, and the sidewalks became more congested. He witnessed a colored man, in a maroon tailored suit, sweet-talking a young woman of the same race, wrapped deep in a faux-fur coat. The woman leaned with her back against a lamp post, as the man leaned close towards her. While both seemed happy with the situation, neither seemed particularly obsessed, or especially desirous. To Will, this appeared to be a case of common garden flirtation. And so the amateur sleuth continued North. The weather worked against his mission; and he found himself wishing it were mid-spring, when love is, as they say, in the air. He anticipated that Central Park would be a cornucopia of options and opportunities for surreptitiously claiming objects brushed by the pagan gods of romance. But he would have to wait at least two months until he could take advantage of such abundance; something he was not keen to do, now that he had started along this road.

Will soon found himself in Herald Square, and when a soft rain began to fall, he darted across the slick road and into Macy's department store. Here he became distracted by all the products and displays, wondering, for a moment, if he could fool Madame Gavorski by procuring something from the shelves here, and claiming they were poached in the midst of a clandestine rendezvous. This would certainly save time. But even if the psychic were fooled, the spell would surely be compromised. At this thought, Will scoffed to himself, at his own superstition. But even as he did so, he knew that he would stick faithfully to the instructions, for fear of spoiling the process. After riding the slow wooden escalator to the second floor, Will found himself in the ladies' shoe department. Here he came upon two women in their late twenties, perhaps in from Jersey for the day, judging by their accents. One was trying on "evening" shoes, and asking her friend for advice.

"Harry will adore these," she said to her friend, with a wink. "I don't know what it is, but as soon as I put a pair of shoes on — anything but my fluffy slippers — he becomes like a puppy or somethin'. Even if they are just my regular work shoes."

Will tried to look inconspicuous as possible, as he eavesdropped on the conversation. The woman continued, oblivious to his presence:

"...but you know, I have two pairs of extra fancy stilettos, good enough for Lana Turner. An' if I put those on — oh brother! — I have the poor guy eatin' out of my hand for a week. It's like he's gonna faint or somethin'. Makes me feel like an angel. An' the kicker is, he looks so *grateful*."

The woman's friend giggled, and then chimed in. "Oh I wish I had someone like that. My Jimmy would just say, 'you look too tall now — watcha tryin' to do? Make me look bad?'" and tell me to put on my flats if I know what's good for me."

Five minutes later, Will was back out on the street, trying not to break into a run through the puddles that had already formed around the cross-walks. He had one of the women's pumps under his coat, nestled beneath his hammering heart. (The woman who could make "Harry" weak at the knees, just by putting on some high heels.) The theft had been remarkably easy, given that the women were browsing with their own shoes abandoned on the floor, already half-forgotten in the distracted lust for new footwear. Somehow Will had also managed to avoid being tailed by a store detective. But it wasn't until he had walked maybe ten blocks without someone grabbing him by the arm before he stopped sweating, and began to breathe normally once more. He felt ashamed. He felt alive. He felt a thrill. And he felt ashamed once more. Once Will's racing heart returned to its normal rate, he took a moment to hope that the store would provide the woman with a new pair of pumps for her to wear on the journey home, given that they failed to stop a shoe thief in their own establishment.

The unfamiliar feelings — both emotional and physiological — inspired by this misadventure tapered into a sharp point in Will's core, and he realized he was famished. After deciding against a couple of forsaken chop suey joints, Will chose a cozy Polish café to have lunch. This establishment was much larger than it appeared from the outside, a narrow entrance funneling customers into to a warren of small rooms, and two or three larger ones with communal tables. Inside, immigrant workers of all stations — some in suits, others in coveralls — were eating hearty soups, some pensively, others in good humor. The air was thick with cigarette smoke. Will spied a couple in a booth who seemed to be hungrier for each other than for anything on the menu; and, with some quick and deft movement, was able to install himself at the next table without making himself too conspicuous. He ordered some sausage and mashed potato, and then pretended to read a Polish newspaper he had plucked from a chair for this purpose. Peering over the top of the smudged broadsheet, Will observed the couple as closely as he could; feeling perverse in the process, but also determined to continue with his quest, now he had reached a point of no return. The woman had loose blonde curls, and reminded him a little of Barbara Stanwyck, though it was difficult to get a good look at her features, given how ardently she pressed it near her companion's face and chest. The man was wearing a light sports jacket, and she kept grabbing his collar, and pulling him closer into a kiss, before withdrawing, staring at him silently with swirling eyes, and then sighing, and pressing her forehead against his chest. The man would then inhale the scent of her hair, lost in his own languid thoughts. Some of the other customers pointed their cutlery in the direction of this couple, while continuing to chew with gusto, raising their eyebrows suggestively. The man then looked at his consort with an almost blank intensity, breathing more than speaking short, urgent words. The couple had ordered food, but hardly touched it. Will thought he caught the words, "…but it's only twelve-thirty," before their conversation melted once more into inaudible exhalations. The woman frowned a pretty little frown at what her lover was saying, then brightening in a flash, with a fingernail between her front teeth, when he said something else. Watching her half-shrouded expression was like watching the light change over a field, as clouds pass quickly across the sun. The man kissed his companion's neck three times, slowly and deliberately, as the woman closed her eyes and clenched her diminutive hands into little tight balls between each one; loosening and tightening again, like a visible pulse. This couple may as well have been in their own universe. After glancing at his watch, the man then sprang into action, sweeping his hat off the hook nearby, throwing some crumpled bank notes onto the table, and scooping his lover out of the booth by her waist. Clearly this man knew how to behave around the opposite sex, so that they found him magnetic. The woman quickly opened a pocket mirror, and reapplied her lipstick, while the man put on his coat, and then helped her with hers, in one fluid motion. And when the lovers departed, one of the customers — a portly man, who was likely the class clown as a boy — raised his eyebrows suggestively, before making a confident assertion in Polish to the room, eliciting snorts and chortles from his fellow diners.

Will tried his best to not look like a hobo, as he walked up to the uncleared table, and plucked a strawberry from the young woman's plate. This strawberry had been abandoned on top of her untouched pancakes after a simple bite, so that half was missing, clear enough to leave some dental information in its tangy flesh. Surely this was an almost-Biblical symbol of appetite. Surely this was desire incarnate, thought Will, and tucked the demi-strawberry into his other coat pocket. Once he returned to his table, Will noticed that a po-faced waitress witnessed this act. Indeed, her expression would haunt Will for several days after the fact. Nevertheless, he understood that he was part of a bigger calling now, and would clearly have to endure some humiliation because of it. Indeed, Will felt a queer sense of confidence as he thanked the waitress with a clear voice when his meal arrived, via her wary (and wiry) hands. She scuttled away as fast as she could without causing explicit offense.

Once his stomach was satisfied, Will turned his mind to the third "trophy" to be wrested from the denizens of this chilly city: an object touched somehow by a loving declaration. Stepping out of the windowless, smoke-filled restaurant, Will discovered that the fog had lifted. The sun was dazzling, despite its relative distance from the earth, measured not with the tools of astronomy or geometry, but with the senses under his prickling skin. With no sense of where to seek the trace of an amorous confession, Will continued North. After peering inside countless storefronts, he began to feel mid-afternoon fatigue tug at his sleeve. A siesta would have been welcomed, but he was a long way from his modest mattress, currently waiting patiently in a splash of sunlight through his apartment window. After buying some lukewarm, and exceedingly bitter, coffee from a corner cart, and drinking it swiftly down, Will noticed he was approaching the main branch of the New York Public Library. A large sign draped across the face of the building beckoned him in: "Come Read Between the Lions." Perhaps it was his training as a soldier that made the young man follow the instructions of fortune-tellers and anonymous civic signs alike, but he walked through the two leonine statues, and up the steep steps into the library, which welcomed him with warmer air, and an ambient, stony, echoing hush.

Will ascended more stairs to the Rose Reading Room, and settled into a free chair with a curved green reading lamp. Resting his eyes a while, he managed to drift off for a few minutes; the occasional cough or muffled thudding book lulling him deeper into drowsiness, despite the harsh caffeine buzzing in his veins. When his eyelids lifted once more, he contemplated the painting on the ceiling for a while, with its peach-colored fluffy Renaissance clouds — the poor man's Sistine Chapel — before turning his refreshed attention to his fellow men and women. As to be expected, he was surrounded by many types: students, professors, amateurs, professionals, bored housewives, ambitious autodidacts (as well as ambitious housewives and bored autodidacts), and also the occasional tourist, homeless person, and face-twitching, throat-clearing lunatic.

Will scanned all these faces, in search of signs of being love-struck or heart-sick, but no obvious candidates revealed themselves on first inspection. An older gentleman in a paisley cravat seemed more intent in dislodging something from his ear, than reading the sizable stack of books on the Napoleonic wars that he had gathered from the shelves. A teenage bobbysoxer in a pastel blue sweater peered through the kind of cat's eye bifocals that Marilyn Monroe wears when playfully mimicking an intellectual. This girl was either reading something disguised inside a bigger book, with a large Arabic title embossed in gold, or else she was an unusual and precocious polyglot. Will spent several minutes watching this not wholly wholesome specimen chew gum and blow small pink bubbles as she read with great focus; skillfully popping them back into her mouth in a soundless manner, in subconscious deference to her environment. This girl was too absorbed to notice the young man's attention, as her jaw slowed to a touching stillness when something in her book monopolized her attention, both body and mind. But Will could not justify further observation, when it was clear that this young creature may indeed have had a vivid and sympathetic imagination, but nothing pressing to declare.

After moving from chair to chair for a while, a middle-aged man's visage and demeanor caught Will's attention. The man was bald, and not especially dignified. Nor did he exhibit the outward appearance of anything inviting stigma. Perhaps he was an accountant, or middle-manager. His face or clothing would have been hard-pressed to recall in any detail, only a minute or two after experiencing them. As Will took further notice of this particular patron of the great library, he could feel his memory rejecting the man's features, even as they registered as neither especially pleasant or unpleasant. And yet Will could sense that this anonymous person's soul was in turmoil. He could feel, with almost a telepathic certainty, that this fellow was wracked with emotions that could no longer be bottled up inside. The man's eyes were watery, a tear or two caught in the corners of his eye (patted away as inconspicuously as possible, with a checkered handkerchief). The man's limbs were somewhat agitated, and his yellow teeth gnawed nervously on his lower lip, under which bristled a trimmed grey beard. He was composing something on expensive writing paper; most likely a love letter, from the silent intensity that was being decanted haltingly from the core of his being and on to the lavender-colored stationary before him. Will waited patiently, as a hunter sits stock-still for hours near a watering hole, waiting for a tiger or elephant to quit drinking, and wander in his direction. Eventually the man did the equivalent of such a decisive movement, signing the letter with an unexpected flourish, as if to seal the message with an inky kiss. He then emitted a profound sigh, perhaps deliberately delivering the letter to the caprice of the Gods, as much as to the beloved that he currently held so dear in his mind.

Will suddenly felt weary of stealing, and, in honor of this fellow's hopeful distress, decided for a direct approach.

"Excuse me sir," he whispered, startling the gentleman into an unfocused attention. "I'm sorry to bother you, but may I borrow your pen."

The man seemed as confused as someone suddenly wrenched out of a dream, and took a few beats to return to the social world.

"Yes, of course," he replied, handing the writing instrument to Will, with a moment's hesitation. Will noticed from the mark that this pen had already been taken from an insurance company. Ironic, he thought to himself, given how little insurance one can have in matters of love.

"Thank you," said Will, with a slight bow, before turning on his heel, and walking out of the Rose Room, and down the spacious stairway, and out into the wintry twilight of New York at the homecoming rush hour. On the busy subway, riding back downtown, Will could still feel the man's surprised eyes boring into the back of his head; even as Will had resisted turning back to actually see them.

Two hours later, Will returned to Madame Gavorski's, only to find a young woman he did not recognize, standing at the threshold. She was slender, pale, and of a melancholy demeanor, wearing garments that a gypsy bride might wear, the day before her wedding.

"Oh, I'm sorry," Will said, taken aback. "I'm looking for the psychic."

"That is me," said the young woman, without conviction.

"Oh no. I mean the *other* psychic. An older woman. She is usually sitting there in the window."

"That is me," repeated the young woman, unblinking.

A long pause filled the room like a plume of invisible smoke, before the young woman continued.

"I am Madame Gavorski," she added, in a tone that one might use on a slow child. "I did not tell you during your last visit, but I am a shape-shifter." The young woman smiled for the first time, becoming infinitely more attractive as she did so. "You are lucky I did not decide to be a cat today. You must have seen me basking in the window sometimes."

Will smiled in return, to convey that he now understood, and appreciated, what surely must be a joke.

"Ah ok. *Now* I understand," said Will, in a conspiratorial tone. "And when *was* my last visit, do you remember?" he asked, to test the preposterous story.

"Last night," she replied, again without blinking. "You paid me ten dollars for a love spell."

Will's smile stumbled a little, before finding its feet again among his other features; as if to say: "Ok. Clearly the two of you are in on this trick, somehow, but I'm going to be a good sport about it."

"Did you bring the three objects?" she asked.

"I…I did," replied Will.

"Come. Sit down. Show me," she said, gesturing to the same chair that the young man had sat upon the night before. Will then proceeded to remove the shoe, the half-strawberry, and the pen from his coat pockets, and place them on the small table between them, with an expression equally torn between the sheepish and the proud. The now-young Madame Gavorski took the first object by the heel, the next by the green stem, and the last by the base, and examined them closely, one by one. As she did so, Will could hear the indistinct murmerings of a radio play coming from the other room.

"Interesting," the wrinkle-free fortune teller said, after a while. "Obsession, appetite, and declaration. Good. Just as I instructed."

Will nodded, pleased with this praise, even as the situation was still rather perplexing to him.

"Tell me," she said. "The person who bit into this strawberry. Was that a woman?"

"Yes."

"And was she beautiful?"

"Depressingly so, yes," replied Will.

"Good.... And you still have the stone under your pillow?"

"Yes. I do."

"Also good. One more expedition for you, then. And three more items to find. Then I will have enough to bend your fortune towards a different fate."

"You mean a spell?" asked Will.

The young woman smiled, ever so faintly. "I suppose you could call it that. But fortune tellers work differently from witches. Two different crafts, often seeking similar outcomes. I do not practice magic, per se. But I *can* see, and read, supernatural forces. And, if the conditions are right, I can encourage them to flow differently: from the past, through the present, and into the future. That is to say, I can persuade them to flow...otherwise."

"I see," said Will, not convinced he could.

The young woman turned the conversation to the nearest of futures.

"So...tomorrow..."

Will shifted in his chair, better to receive his new instructions.

"…Tomorrow you will return with three more trophies — three more mute witnesses to love. Then I shall have enough to work with."

Will leaned forward, eager to hear the details from her soft-spoken lips.

"First," said the young woman, "*waiting*. Bring me a memento from one who waits."

Will himself waited for more information.

"…All lovers wait. Indeed, lovers know better than any other what it means to wait; how it feels to be pinned to the spot like a butterfly, suspended every breath."

The young woman inhaled rather sharply, rib cage expanding; as if recalling something, before resuming her instructions.

"Second," she listed. "*Seduction*. Bring me something from the bosom of seduction. It matters not if from the seducer or the seduced."

Will took clear mental notes, knowing he would not forget a word (in sharp contrast to those college lectures, which seemed so dry and remote to him now).

"Third and final object," continued the psychic, "*surrender*. Bring back something from the brink of mutual abandonment; from the scene of vouchsafing oneself to another; body and soul."

At this final, rather emphatic, directive, the young woman's eyes flashed. It appeared that she was now looking more inward, than at her client.

For an extended moment, Will suffered an urge to reach out, and take the fortune teller's pale hand. But something about her manner forbade it; as well as the semi-professional relationship which connected them. Truth be told, there was a part of Will that was indeed convinced that he was still sitting opposite the former, older, Madame Gavorski. And he would not have dreamed of doing such a thing in that case. Somewhere in his overstimulated psyche was a small boy, afraid that if he made any gesture of desire — let along loving — the younger woman might suddenly transform into the older, as in a German folk-tale, and cackle at his folly.

And so, Will bid this enigmatic presence goodbye — to which she simply inclined her head in a subtle act of acknowledgement — and returned to his apartment, exhausted.

* * *

That night, Will slept more deeply than at any other time since his return from the war. His bones felt the same kind of leaden weight from hours upon hours of watching and waiting in high alert, senses stretched along a thin invisible string of adrenalin; albeit without the fear of sudden death robbing the chest of breath. He dreamed in slow, pluming charcoal shapes, illuminated by sudden flares of turquoise. These shapes suggested isolated beings, which would collapse around and into each other, like different ink pots, spilled over the same piece of parchment; only to trickle and flow into separate shapes and directions once again. The inside of his skull pulsed with sexless, but blood-quickened, cave paintings, animating themselves in the subterranean dark; awaiting a struck match for revelation or witness.

When the morning sun splashed his face awake, Will took a few moments to remember not only where he was, but who he was. Once this task was accomplished, with more effort than usual, the young man wished he had not spent the full ten dollars on the fortune teller. In that case, he could have ordered a full breakfast in the diner below. As it was, he was forced to be frugal, and eat five slices of spongey white bodega bread, and as much of an over-ripe banana as he could stomach. Then, after a reviving shower, Will dressed for another morning of possibly schizophrenic weather, and stepped out and back into the diner for the coffee that would reintegrate him fully into the flow of a new day.

Now that some successful questing was behind him, the three new challenges did not seem so abstract or intimidating. Indeed, it struck Will just how quickly and unquestioningly human beings can adapt to new instructions, no matter how strange or irrational. "Take that ridge." "Yes, sir." "Kill those men." "Yes, sir." "Pocket that evidence of a loving heart." "Yes, ma'am."

Yesterday's rather improvised and serendipitous series of en-
counters, gave way to a more strategic approach. For *waiting,*
Will deliberately targeted Grand Central Station. Once there,
watching from above on the second level, like a fleshy gargoyle,
he almost immediately spotted a red-headed woman in her
thirties, pacing impatiently back and forth, and watching the
arrivals board with rather feverish eyes. She wore a short fur
coat, a small hat with netting over half her freckled face, and a
rich green satin skirt. What caught Will's eye was the way that
she was distractedly pulling a matching green silk scarf through
her long pale fingers; up and over each separate finger, like the
prelude to a magic trick. Taken all together, this woman's body
language cried out in the stifled anguish of a lover, trapped in
public, obliged to attend the messianic arrival of her beloved.
Will could feel his own heart quicken in anticipation; so that
when the gentleman in question finally arrived — surprisingly
perhaps, a good foot shorter than she was, and somewhat portly, albeit with a mischievously attractive face — Will shared in a
portion of the relief which flushed her pale cheeks. The couple
were so absorbed in each other, once they had moved arm in
arm to the Oyster Bar, that Will needed only to saunter smoothly past their table in order to pilfer her green silk scarf, and push
it into his front pocket, like a formal handkerchief.

Seduction proved almost *too* easy, as Will figured that he
need only go to Bloomingdale's perfume counter to catch this
very deliberate staging of the self in progress. Here he encountered a gentleman in a striped sports jacket, and a carnation
in his button hole, scrutinizing the various bottled fragrances
with more attention and knowledge than any woman of leisure
may have done. Something about the gentleman's manner-
isms — along with his grey pompadour, and impeccably short
and sharp moustache — suggested to the younger man that the
seduction planned may not involve the fair sex at all. For a moment Will feared that, if true, such an inversion may warp the
fortune teller's capacity to bend events in his favor with the ladies. Will soon reasoned, however, that the heart can also be a
very pragmatic organ. And he decided to take the risk, in order

to keep the momentum of this unorthodox treasure hunt going. On this occasion there was no fear of the store detectives, since the young man merely swiped one of the heavy-embossed paper samples that the charismatic gentleman placed on the counter, having inhaled its scent deeply, while placing his elegant right hand over his heart, and nodding to the woman behind the counter with an expression that seemed to already partake of the bliss that it promised.

Surrender, however, proved more elusive, as it is not something usually practiced outdoors or in public. Indeed, Will spent a fruitless afternoon haunting second-hand book stores and disreputable licensed spaces around Times Square, in search of such a rare and singular motion. Here instead he found gestures of exhibition and extroversion, performance and perversion, beckoning and reckoning, lasciviousness and obliviousness, shamelessness and shame; but nothing even remotely reminiscent of a yielding to love. And so he moved to hotel lobbies and bars, where he caught the scent of his mark, but not its face, or even shadow. Eventually, Will returned to his own neighborhood, and a dark coffee house, known as The Nomad, that held poetry evenings and folk singers, serving cheap and clandestine Greek wine in chipped tin mugs after 8pm. Here Will found an obscure corner at a rickety wooden table, and returned to *Women in Love,* squinting in the dim candle-light, glancing around the room for any promising signs, before turning each page. Even in such a distracted state, Will was struck with how much more real and immediate the novel now felt to him; as vivid as any of his recent adventures. It was as if it had become a completely different book, thanks to the intervention of the fortune teller on Bleeker Street.

A few tedious minutes after an earnest young man took the tiny stage, and started to strum a badly tuned guitar, a couple entered, bringing a heightened state of existence with them. Equally portioned between them, they boasted the kind of beauty that demands the company of the same, perhaps more ornate than consequential. If forced to guess, one may hazard that they were French or Swedish, visiting New York for reasons of their own, as they appeared to be refugees from the stylish art films that excited some of Will's college companions so. The man was wearing a black turtleneck, and the woman a maroon beret that matched her lipstick. They stood by the counter for a while, and ordered some wine. When a table became free, no-one disputed their right to take it. Will then watched, as the man made several attempts to kiss her, but she parried them all away, clearly on the edge of succumbing to his charms. Perhaps they had quarreled recently, and she was punishing him still, for as long as she could resist. But it was clear that she was on the brink of yielding. As he watched, Will almost summoned his own incantations, under his breath, to encourage her to do so, even as he was unsure what his trophy would be if she did. The tin cup perhaps?

But then fate once more went out of its way to point to a specific object: this time an almost Egyptian-looking silver ear-ring, which — on closer inspection — appeared to be a stylized archer, framing a large piece of jade, inlaid with pearl. The woman's fingers played rather obsessively with this object, as the man whispered words in her opposite ear, in whatever language they shared, each breath bringing her closer to assenting to something he demanded with his every twitch. As if infused with the spirit of two courting birds, the man used his arms like strong wings to claim the space around her, and she, in turn, swiveled her elegant neck. She then tilted her face upwards, to meet his looming gaze from above. Together like this, in the red shadows of the smoke-filled coffee shop, one could be forgiven for thinking these two patrons were indeed exotic birds, tapping their beaks together in place of asking explicit questions. At the sudden softening of her alert body, Will noticed the precise moment of surrender; a decisive transition marked by the fact that her earring clattered to the floor, unnoticed by anyone else; least of all the woman herself, as their mouths met and hungered.

By the time Will emerged from the smoky establishment, with all his mementos in his pockets, it was only forty-five minutes away from the midnight chime. Nevertheless, he felt so energized by his quest, and so impatient to give his fresh relics to the fortune teller, that he walked the four blocks to the storefront, and was relieved to see the neon sign still lit. Peering through the window, Will could not see any life inside, but after buzzing three times, the door opened. After an uncanny moment, in which Will saw no presence whatsoever, he looked down to find a young girl of no more than nine years old. She too, however, was dressed like a gypsy for a festive occasion. And she too welcomed him as if they were already well acquainted.

"Ah," she said, in a deeper voice than one might expect from such a fragile body. "You have returned already. Our young soldier, student, and lover."

Will smiled, somewhat uncertainly, his system sluggish with cheap fermented Greek grapes.

"Don't tell me," he said, leaning closer, as adults tend to do when talking to small children they don't know. "You are also Madame Gavorski?"

"Correct," said the diminutive psychic, who then made a preternaturally adult and gracious gesture with her arm, to welcome him deeper into the parlor: a motion so natural as to seem supremely practiced (or perhaps the other way around).

Earlier that day, the young man had been curious which of the two Madame Gavorski's he would be meeting next. But the possibility of yet another — and younger still — had not entered his mind.

"Do you have your three objects?" the girl asked, once they had settled on opposite sides of the same table.

"I do," answered Will, unable to keep the note of pride from creeping into his voice, and placing them one by one on the somewhat stained gold tablecloth. Some slow big-band jazz, with radio static, wafted in from a hidden room, and the scent of chicken stock floated in and out of Will's nostrils.

The tiny Madame Gavorski observed each item one by one, through a little eyepiece designed for close examination. She then clicked her tongue in approval, and tied the green scarf around her delicate neck, and removed a small silver stud from her left ear lobe, and hung the amber earring, which was too large for her elfin head.

"Very good," said the gypsy girl, locking Will's shifting gaze with her sad, serene, and bottomless brown eyes. "You have fulfilled your part of the process. Tonight, I will do mine. And tomorrow," she paused, for dramatic effect. "Tomorrow, you will find that the words of love come easier to your lips. You will find that the movements of your limbs will more confidently shape the amorous dance of bodies. You will find that your eyes see with more clarity the rebuffs that are real, and the ones designed to encourage you to continue. You will, in short, find the art and business of love to be something you now approach with a new understanding, and ease."

Will noticed that this little speech was delivered with eyes lowered, perhaps even read off a card beneath the table. But he found the message too heartening to explicitly question the legitimacy of its source. The young girl continued:

"Now that you have paid special attention to specific gestures of love, you will recognize them more easily, and execute them yourself, with more confidence."

Will nodded, feeling the truth of this claim.

"What is more, you will have a new appreciation for the fact that love is a myth, *made real* through actions. The heart fashions love from what it can find. One makes love with the materials to hand."

Having delivered this little speech, the young girl interlaced her delicate fingers and lay her hands on the table, as if to put a final punctuation on this lesson; returning her gaze to his. Will stared at the young girl's large, almost bovine eyes, wondering how to respond to such wisdom, delivered from the naïve lips of a child.

"So that's it?" he asked, almost disappointed. "I can go now, and things will be better?"

His uncanny companion bowed her head slowly, her eyes closing as she did so, like those sleepy dolls, in assent. With equal grace, the girl extended her left hand and opened her palm, as if waiting for payment, as she continued to look demurely at the table top.

Will balked, then said with some indignance.

"Madame Gavorski told me that my initial payment would be enough."

The girl continued to look at the table, tiny hand outstretched, like a modest supplicant, before replying: "But *I* am Madame Gavorski. And I welcome all sundry compensations for the efforts of reshaping the future, on a kind young man's behalf."

Will had faced many foes back in Korea, but none as devious and forceful as this. And so, he fished around in his pocket, and produced three single dollars, and placed them in the girl's hand, which suddenly curled up around the crumpled bills, like a sensitive sea plant, capturing a passing fish.

Will then bade the psychic goodnight, and returned to his apartment, feeling somewhat foolish once again, for having taken this recent experience at face value. Nevertheless, he continued to sleep with the turquoise stone under his pillow. Until, that is, one of the young women from his "Eros and Literature" class found it the following week, between love-making sessions, and asked if she could keep it.

Will could never say for sure whether the fortune teller had intervened in the flow of his future on his behalf, or if the experience alone had given him a more sensitive sense of the choreography of passion (and thus an advantage in adapting this for his own performance of its gestures). The young man felt it unwise to decide either way, for fear of jinxing the effects in any case.

All that he knew was that he was happy: sitting in the booth of this diner, on a warm Spring morning, cherry blossoms bursting on the trees out the window; his new girlfriend teasing him about his opinions on British novelists, while wearing his favorite sweater, and sipping coffee out of a soup bowl (as she insisted on ordering). He knew he was happy; glimpsing the love bite that peeped out from the top of this sweater; a crimson dab of the figurative brush which physical passion uses in order to paint love into existence. He knew he was happy, when he saw the three women walking slowly home together, on the other side of the road, wearing ordinary American clothes — one old and plump, one young and slim, the other a mere child — each carrying grocery bags, one filled with soup cans, each pensively ignoring the presence of the others, no doubt dreaming their own daydreams of love: one long gone, one in motion, and the other, yet to come.